I0653554

Recruited

T.S.O. Bk 3

R.E. Klinzing

T.S.O. Series

Finding Doom

The Bayshire

Recruited

A Hostage in Headquarters

BAYSHIRE
PUBLICATIONS

The characters and events portrayed in this book are fictitious. Any similarity to events or real persons, living or dead, is coincidental and not intended by the author.

Text Copyright 2025
All Rights Reserved

R.E. Klinzing
Recruited

No part of this publication may be reproduced, stored in a retrieval system, or transmitted in any form or by any means electronic, mechanical, photocopying, recording, or otherwise without the prior permission of the publisher.

Published by: Bayshire Publications
Cover design by R.E. Klinzing

ISBN: 978-1-7373043-4-0
eBook ISBN: 978-1-7373043-5-7

reklinzing.com

For every child that's pretended to be a spy.
Never stop working towards your goals. I'm rooting
for you!

Recruited

Chapter 1

Busted

It might be silly or childish, but I don't care. I typed in the last part of the code I was working on and activated it. My pranks were getting better, more advanced, more dynamic. The next time Emily Steinfeld turned on her computer, dozens of popups would cover her laptop advertising whipped cream. Then her screen would glitch, causing the page to go blank. It would only stay up for a minute, then a notification would pop up with a note from me telling her she's been hacked by Yours Truly. I shut off my computer just before my father walked into the kitchen.

"What are you doing?" he asked. He wore a casual tan suit over a white button-down shirt and gray tie. How could he wear the same thing every day and never grow tired of it?

"Just getting ready for school," I said, shoving my homework into my backpack.

"Those math equations better be right this time, you hear me?" His voice was cold, as usual, his eyes never once met my face. I rolled my eyes. "I'm serious, Tony. One more bad grade from you and I'm taking away your computer."

"Daaad!" I groaned.

"Tony Anderson, don't talk back to me, understand?" I nodded, my back to the old man. Dad grabbed his briefcase from the kitchen counter, his car keys from the hook on the wall, and headed to the front door. "Don't be late for school." And with those impeccable fatherly words of advice, he slammed the door behind him.

"Understand, Tony?" I mumbled. "I understand perfectly!" I grabbed a muffin from the fridge, slung my bag over my shoulder, and left the house just as the bus stopped at the curb.

Out in the school parking lot, I spotted one of my best friends as she headed towards class. I ran to catch up with her. "Hey Zegro." Amelia Zegro turned to me and smiled. I smiled back, unable to stop myself. Amelia was amazing, the way her blonde hair fell around her shoulders, how the sunlight made her cheeks glow, the way she smiled. I glanced down at the brace on her knee.

Amelia was in a car accident a little while ago. She seriously injured her knee, but it was healing fast. They said she was suffering from partial memory loss. The thought terrified me, but I didn't notice any differences about her.

"Heard you're getting your brace off tomorrow, must be exciting," I said, meeting her blue eyes. Sure, she seemed a little more cautious, more on-guard. But Amelia has always been like that.

"Definitely," she said, those eyes brightening even more. "You ready for your prank on Emily?" she asked. I smirked. I had been working on this since before her accident. Amelia was the only person who knew about it. My other friends would have given it away. I was calling it "My prank of the year." The last prank I pulled on Emily involved her entire desk being filled with whipped cream. That one didn't end too well, but hopefully this one will be less harmful. I was intent on making whipped cream a theme.

"I wonder what her face will look like." I imagined Emily's shock, her dropped jaw and her scrunched up nose once she realized what I did. I could never prank Amelia. She couldn't handle a joke as well as Emily, she was a little too uptight for that. Not to mention she would see it coming long before I even hatched a plan. "I've got to get to class," I said. "See you later."

"I hope it isn't too serious!" Amelia shouted. I smiled to myself. You could always count on Amelia Zegro to be cautious, but she was the one that kept me out of trouble. As long as I didn't get caught, everything would work out fine.

Later in the day, some kids mulled around the picnic tables while others darted for the field during lunch break. I stood with Amelia near the lunch tables. Emily made her way over to us. She stormed right past Amelia, pointing a finger at my chest.

"Why would you do that?" Emily shouted at me. I bent over laughing, I couldn't help it. Her expression was perfect, her nose scrunched up, her hair frazzled. "You scared me, I thought I erased my homework. My mom's computer was hacked yesterday!"

I muffled a laugh. "Sorry, Emily. I thought it would be funny. Amelia and I got a kick out of it." At that moment Amelia tapped Emily on the shoulder and made her jump. I laughed even harder. Amelia said something, but I didn't catch it. I was too busy trying to stop laughing.

Emily finally calmed down and started laughing with us. The look of anger dissipated. "Whose computer was hacked?" Amelia asked, more forcefully now.

"My mom's computer. I don't know who did it." Emily crossed her arms and glared at me. It wasn't very convincing as her smile escaped her lips.

I put my hands up in surrender. "Hey, at least I didn't get caught this time." I laughed again, and Emily shook her head at me.

"Oh, you just wait," she said.

"Wait for what, our new homeroom teacher to rat me out? It's not like Ms. Blanchard has any idea what any of us are like." I glanced at Amelia. She was spaced out, her thoughts elsewhere. She gave us a little look and headed off, probably to her choir practice.

"I wouldn't be too sure about that," Emily said. She gestured behind me.

"What do you mean?" I asked. Emily nodded behind me again, and I turned around. Our new teacher, Ms. Blanchard, stood across the parking lot, her hand at her hip, and stared at me. She didn't look angry, which was even more disturbing.

"Good luck," Emily said. "I hear she's pretty strict." Emily smiled, patted my shoulder, and walked away.

I brushed my hand through my thick, black hair and stared at Ms. Blanchard. So much for not getting caught.

Chapter 2

Recruited

Ms. Blanchard walked towards me, her heels clacking against the cement. "Hi Ms. Blanchard," I said with a weak smile.

"This way, Anderson." Ms. Blanchard turned around and walked away, her curls bobbing with each step. Most teachers would just send me to the principal's office. This felt much more dangerous.

A couple of months ago, right around the time of Amelia's accident, Ms. Blanchard became our new eighth grade teacher. No one said anything about it. Our last teacher was gone for reasons that were not shared with us and Ms. Blanchard took over for the rest of the school year.

"Where are we going?" I asked, speeding up to catch up with her.

"My office." The thought of Ms. Blanchard and my father in the same room made me shudder.

I was expecting to be led to a teacher's office, but she took me to the classroom instead.

"You know this isn't your office, right?" I asked. Or was it?

Ms. Blanchard glared at me. "Sit down, Anderson."

"Who's that?" I asked, spotting the man sitting in the back of the classroom.

"An associate. Don't worry about him."

I gulped and sat at one of the desks in the front row. Ms. Blanchard closed the classroom door and pulled down the blinds on the little window. She strolled over to me, gave me a curious look, then sat at her desk.

The man in the corner didn't move, didn't say a word. I turned back to my teacher.

"So," Ms. Blanchard started, folding her hands together on her desk. "How did you manage to hack into Emily's computer?"

"Well, it was a little tricky until I bypassed all her passwords," I said, slouching in my chair, glancing at the locked door. Did she want me to really tell her how I did it? Should I be defending myself right now? Where was Amelia when I needed her? "Are you going to tell my dad?" I asked. I crossed my arms. "Because if you are, he probably won't answer until he's out of work. He doesn't like to be bothered by issues that concern me," I said.

"That depends on this conversation."

"Really?" Ms. Blanchard didn't answer. I frowned at her. "You're not like other teachers, are you?"

"Mr. Anderson, we've been watching you for some time now." She leaned forward in her seat.

"What is that supposed to mean?" I asked, shifting in my seat. She was definitely not a normal teacher.

"It means we see potential in you. Tony, you have good skills that are being wasted. Do you really want to be doing silly pranks and getting into trouble for the rest of your life?"

"Is this supposed to be some sort of new therapy for acting out?" I asked. "Because if it is, it's not going to work."

"You need to stop fooling around Anderson, or this world is going to make life a lot more difficult for you. I have an offer for you." I opened my mouth to say something, but she cut me off. "Now, before you start talking back, hear me out. I'm not just a teacher."

"That's for sure," I muttered, rolling my eyes.

Ms. Blanchard didn't react to my comment. "Tony, I run a very important, very secret underground agency. It's called the Teen Spy Organization, or the T.S.O. for short. I'm not messing with you, and I'm not punishing you. I'm giving you a one-time offer to join my organization. We could use someone with your skillset in the field or in mission control."

"Wait, hold on a second." I sat up straighter. "What exactly are you talking about here?"

"Tony, what I'm talking about is a secret spy agency run across the country. I am one of the directors. The T.S.O. is a secret organization that aims to stop crime and protect the citizens of this fine country. We recruit all our agents as teenagers, believing it will give you the upper hand in the field, seeing as most people don't look for teenagers fighting crime. We only recruit the best and the brightest."

Ms. Blanchard stared at me. She wasn't kidding about this. Her eyes locked on mine. I looked away to relieve the tension, thinking over what this all meant. It made more sense than this woman being an eighth-grade teacher.

"If you only take the best and the brightest, then why tell me all of this?"

"Tony, I've been watching you. You're smart. For some reason, you just decide not to do your homework right. You have skills other kids don't even know exist. That prank you pulled today was the last thing I was waiting for. If Emily Steinfeld believed you had hacked her, which in a way you did, then I know your skills are exactly what I'm looking for. I'm never wrong about things like this."

"So, you're actually asking me to join a secret spy organization?" I almost shouted the question, millions of thoughts popping into my head. What would my dad think? Me! A secret agent! Who would ever believe something like that?

"This is your only invitation, Tony."

"And what if I don't take it?" I asked, shifting in my seat.

"If you refuse, we'll erase your memory of this ever happening, and you'll go on with your life like this conversation never happened."

"You can erase people's memories?" I asked.

I glanced at Ms. Blanchard's associate in the corner. He didn't move.

"What do you say, Tony?"

Way to dodge the question.

My heel tapped against the floor. I could hear my own breathing as time slowed in my mind. What should I say? On one hand, it seemed like a crazy idea. Teenagers were running around the city as secret agents. It was absurd. There were so many legal issues with that. What if Ms. Blanchard was lying and this whole thing was a trick? If I said yes, I could end up in a locked room somewhere with people planning to do who knew what with me.

Then there was my dad. He would never allow something like this. It wasn't that it sounded dangerous or risky. It wasn't his idea. His plan for my life consisted of ties and board meetings.

On the other hand, the agency was secret for a reason. He never had to know. He hardly paid enough attention to me as it was. If I was careful, I could get away with this whole thing and he would never smell the secret I was cooking. Dad would be none the wiser if I really became a secret agent.

If I said yes, I was opening a door I didn't even knew existed this morning. Maybe everything Mom taught me could really be put to good use. I knew deep down that she would say yes, would want me to say yes.

"Well?" Ms. Blanchard asked. "What's it going to be?"

I looked up at her, a faint smile playing on my lips. If this woman was telling the truth, how could I say no?

This morning, I had nothing exciting to look forward to other than pranking Emily. If I could pull this off, it would really be the prank of a lifetime. Living undercover, stopping crooks, solving crime. My friends would love an opportunity like this.

At that moment, I knew if I turned this down, I would regret it forever.

I met Ms. Blanchard's gaze, leaning forward on my desk.

"I'm in."

Chapter 3

Serving Up Baking Soda

"Hey Tony."

"Hi Patty." I smiled at her, not because she's a great boss and the most kind-hearted person ever, but because I now have a secret. The soup kitchen is always busy, full of bodies eating, laughing, and telling stories. Heading to the employee break room, I tossed my backpack on the floor and pulled my apron over my head.

As a secret agent, everything else I would do would feel like a cover. A ruse. I liked that idea. In a way, this was already a cover. Here no one knew what I was like outside the soup kitchen doors. They only knew the genius I let them know.

When I met Patty back at the counter, I grabbed a large serving spoon and started dishing out rice. "How's your dad doing?" she asked, peeking at me through the corner of her eye.

"He's great," I lied, not bothering to look at her. I started volunteering here almost a year ago. When he got the new promotion at work, Dad said it was his responsibility to entertain clients, which meant a weekly dinner at the house with people I wasn't allowed to meet. Dad said I wasn't allowed to be home during his work dinner, so I didn't "mess anything up," so he set up this volunteer gig to keep me out of the house.

"It's a win-win," he said. "It will look good on your resume and help your future. You should be thanking me." Despite his reasons for making me volunteer here, it really was a blessing. Being home with my father wasn't always a good idea, and the people here were amazing.

"How's it going, Sandy?" I asked when a gray-haired woman stopped in front of me.

"Just fine, Tony. Just fine." She smiled at me before sliding down the counter with a plate full of rice.

If I really had the opportunity to work for the T.S.O., maybe I could make a difference in people's lives. Serving dinner to people was one thing, but fighting crime? That had adventure written all over it. Why the T.S.O. wanted me, I don't know. Sure, I knew a thing or two about computers and chemistry. My mother taught me well before she disappeared, but I was in no way the cool kid who knew how to handle himself. I didn't seem to please anyone of importance in my life. Not my dad, nor my real teachers. My friends saw me as the prankster, someone fun to hang out with. I was never the shoulder to cry on or the one trusted in times of need. I was the entertainment, and I liked it that way. Still, I pictured myself making a difference, beating up bad guys and stopping crooks. Doing something *real*.

"Not again!" The shout came from the kitchen.

"Better go see what happened," Patty said.

"I'll be right back."

Joanna was leaning over the sink pouting. "What's wrong?" I asked.

"It's all clogged again." Joanna frowned at me. "I need these vegetables washed if we're going to serve dinner. Please help. You fixed it last time."

"Not a problem," I said, peering into the water and food filling up the sink. I knew what to do to fix the problem. My mom had shown me how to fix these things a long time ago. I ran boiling water into the sink, grabbed a large bowl off the counter and created a solution with baking soda and vinegar. Before pouring it into the sink I clogged the drain and turned to Joanna. "Give it-"

"A few minutes. I know. Thanks." She smiled at me as she wiped her hands on her apron before I went back to the line. I hoped the T.S.O. training camp would be more exciting than unclogging drains.

My mom was a chemist. On the weekends we would do our own science experiments, and she would teach me about how to use chemicals and other items to solve my problems. She taught me how they interacted with each other, how I could make them work for me. After she left, and Dad became the way he is, her science was the only thing I had left of her. And now I use it to unclog drains. How exciting.

The following day, I couldn't wipe the smile off my face. Nobody noticed anything was different when I got to school. I sat with the guys at the lunch table. "One more!" Wyatt exclaimed, opening his mouth wide. I tossed a grape into his mouth. Everyone laughed. Someone slapped Wyatt on the back. The grape flew out of his mouth and across the table. Laughter exploded from every direction.

"Mr. Anderson." I choked back a laugh. Ms. Blanchard towered over me, a frown playing at her eyebrows.

"Ooh. What did you do now?" Wyatt asked, eliciting laughter once again from the group.

"Yes?" I asked, giving my friends a harsh look.

"Come with me please."

12

"Anderson's in trouble," someone shouted. I sighed and stood from the table. Snickers followed as I trailed behind Ms. Blanchard out of the cafeteria and into the classroom.

"Is this about the whipped cream thing?" I asked, still smiling as I sat at a desk once again. "Because that was yesterday, and you can't prove it was me. Not really."

Ms. Blanchard sighed and sat in front of me. "As much as I don't like your pranks, no. This is not about the whipped cream thing."

"Is this about the secret agent stuff you were talking about?" I asked, the smile gone from my face.

"Yes. This is your last chance to finalize your decision."

"I told you, I'm in." Ms. Blanchard glared at me. "Ma'am."

"I have papers for you to sign and information regarding the start to your official training." I nodded at her. "As I mentioned earlier, we see a lot of potential in you. Before I tell you anything else about myself or about the Teen Spy Organization, I need you to sign these." She slid a file in front of me with a pen.

"These papers say you will never tell anyone the truth about the T.S.O., that we exist, or that you are in any way connected to us. You must agree to complete confidentiality. You are also signing that you are joining our organization under your own free will." I read the papers as she explained them. "There will be more paperwork when you complete your training and become an agent."

"I have a question," I said. She nodded at me. "Do I get paid to be an agent?"

"Of course," she said. "Your earnings will be put into a private savings account. You can access it to draw cash when necessary, but there will be no paper trail of the account or of your employment in any public records outside the T.S.O. database."

"Sweet."

"If you don't have any more questions, go ahead and sign all those papers, then I'll discuss the role I play here and what your training will look like."

I signed the papers, and Ms. Blanchard slid them into a drawer.

"Now, I am a regional director of the Teen Spy Organization. I'm stationed in T.S.O. Headquarters right here in Glayfield, California. I oversee all T.S.O. activity on the West Coast. I also oversee all recruitment. Whenever possible, I like to talk with prospective agents personally, to get to know you and introduce you to our organization like I am doing now."

"So, you're really not a teacher?" I asked.

"No, not quite." She smiled. "As an agent-in-training, you must attend our summer training camp. You are required to attend two years in a row, beginning this summer. It is an eight-week training course. When camp is over, you can take part in continued training on a T.S.O. base. After your second training camp is completed and you pass your certification exam, you can officially start working on cases with a mentor until deemed ready to work solo or with a partner."

"This is a two-year training program?" I asked. It seemed like a long time.

"Yes. You have to understand, you will be trained both physically and mentally to prepare yourself for the field. Even if you end up working in the office, this is the same training every agent must complete. There will be ways for you to train outside of these two summer courses, but the majority of your education will be condensed into these two summers. We find it best to work around school schedules in this way. And like I said, you will get paid after the end of your first training camp, so it can count as a summer job if your parents were to require it."

I frowned at her desk. "I don't think pay would be the problem."

"Tony, the best way to advance your training is at this camp." She enunciated her words with such importance I had to look at her. "You will need parent permission since you will be gone for two months. I can provide whatever you need to encourage your father, but you will have to convince him to let you go to summer camp without telling him what you are actually doing. In a way it will be your first test as an agent."

"And what if I can't?" I asked, wringing my hands together. I couldn't believe the one thing standing in the way of this might be my dad.

Ms. Blanchard thought for a moment, then spoke slowly. "There are other ways we can train you on base, but they are more slow-going. You will have to fit in extra classes outside of your school and personal schedule."

I sighed. "I'll see what I can do."

Chapter 4

Cardboard Cutouts Make Great Friends

"Amelia, wait!" I cried out as I watched Amelia board the city bus. The doors closed before I reached her, and the bus pulled away from the curb. I shrugged my shoulders and kept walking down the street towards home.

It wasn't that I needed to tell her something, that I *could* tell her about the T.S.O. or anything important. I was just going to say hi, but whatever.

"Hey, man." Wyatt trotted over to me from the corner store.

"Hey, Wyatt. What's happening?"

"You want to shoot some hoops or are you too busy chasing girls?"

I smiled. "Not at all." Anything that would keep me from having to go home just yet and tell my father about a fake summer camp. We headed to the park, but we didn't shoot hoops. "Who are we playing with today?" I asked.

Wyatt nodded in the direction of some children on the playground. There were three of them, racing each other down the slides and laughing. By the looks of it, they had to be around seven years old. The parents were at the other end of the playground talking amongst themselves.

"Any ideas?" Wyatt asked.

I thought for a moment, took in everything around me, slipped my backpack off my shoulder and rummaged through it. "Absolutely. You see that cardboard box lying by the trash can? We'll need that."

This is what we did when we were bored, when we didn't want to go home. Wyatt lived with a single mother who was barely home, leaving him alone while she worked afternoon shifts at the hospital. If he wasn't pulling pranks with me, hanging with people from school, he was making his mom's life miserable, always wanting to be the cool kid with a bad attitude. In reality, we played harmless pranks, something that amused us, and eventually made the people we messed with laugh.

I pulled out some scissors and markers from my backpack and we worked on the cardboard, making a mini cutout of a child. When all the folds and slits were in the right place, we were done. We waited for all the kids to gather at the back of the jungle gym and snuck over to the slide. We set up the cardboard child at the bottom of the slide, sitting there waiting for a friend to slide down and take him to the ground.

Wyatt snickered as we huddled behind a fake boulder. After the first kid knocked it down, she was shocked. The little girl turned around, afraid she ran into someone when she slid down the slide. Slowly her fear turned into confusion before giving way to laughter. We laughed with her from our hiding spot.

"What's going on?" A little boy at the top of the slide shouted.

A moment of silence. The little girl scrambled to put the cardboard child back on the slide, failing to hide her snicker.

"Nothing!" she shouted back, laughing to herself. "Come on down."

Like in a slow-motion film, those little boy's eyes widened to the size of oranges when he ran into the cutout. The little girl couldn't stop laughing, and soon he joined in. Wyatt and I laughed from our perch on the rock formation across the jungle gym. Together they tricked the third child into sliding into the cardboard, and it became a game.

"Where have you been?" Dad's voice echoed through the empty halls the moment I stepped foot in the kitchen. He sat at the dining table, eyes glued to his computer, a permanent frown on his forehead.

"Just doing homework," I said.

"You were late for dinner, and now I'm about to go into a business meeting."

I sighed, dropping my bag on the counter. "Sorry."

Dad shook his head, grumbling into his computer. I stared at him for a moment. He didn't even look at me. I had to ask him. It was now or never.

"Hey, Dad?" I pulled the flyers from Ms. Blanchard out. "Hmm."

"Could you pay attention for just a moment? There's something I need to tell you."

"What did you do wrong this time?" he asked, still looking at his laptop.

"Nothing. Listen, there's this summer camp I really want to go to, I just need your permission."

"That isn't going to work. It won't fit into our budget." He leaned closer to his laptop, not paying any attention to me.

"Dad." He waved a hand to dismiss me, all his attention put into his work. Again.

"I'm busy, Tony. Can't you see that? I know you weren't doing homework either, so don't lie to me." He put in an earbud, tuning me out further as he logged into an online meeting.

I clenched my fist. I couldn't get mad. Getting mad always made things worse. It was a specialty of mine. But Mom would think this was important. I had to keep my cool. Ms. Blanchard needed an answer. I let my anger show, just enough to give me the courage I needed. I stood up taller, determined to make myself heard. In a silent prayer, I asked for my mom's guidance, wherever she was. I stepped towards Dad and closed his laptop.

"Tony!" Dad pushed himself back, the chair legs squealing against the wood. "What is wrong with you?"

"I want to tell you about this summer camp."

"What did you do this time?" he shouted, throwing his arms in the air.

"I told you. I didn't do anything."

"I can't believe you, Tony! I thought we were done with the lying and the games."

"No games, there's just this summer camp, and it's really important." I shoved the papers at him, hoping this wasn't a mistake.

He huffed and skimmed through them, shaking his head like the disappointed father he was. The flyers were for a computer science camp in northern California. "Wyatt's mom was pretty angry when she found out you two were scaring kids."

"What? We weren't scaring kids. It was just a little prank, a game!"

At that moment I hated Wyatt for outing us. Of course, he would tell his mom and make it look like he did something cruel. Unlike me, he would do anything for her attention. I needed this. I couldn't spend another summer locked inside these walls with nothing to do.

"You have to stop pulling these pranks, Tony. First you keep running off to hang out with your friends, and now you want me to let you go to some science camp?"

I glared at my shoes. This wasn't going to work. He wasn't going to say yes, and I wouldn't become an agent.

"You're working at the soup kitchen was supposed to help fix your problems, not make them worse!" That wasn't why he made me go there, but no way would I ever tell him that. "Is this really that important?" he shouted. "Answer me, Tony!"

"It's important to me." I said it through clenched jaws, not making eye contact.

"I had to leave a meeting for this!?" He gestures to his shut laptop.

"Dad, I'm sorry."

"It doesn't matter if you're sorry." He shoved the paper back at me and recollected himself, working his fingers through a wrinkle on his forehead. "You know what? Go to this camp for all I care. At least then you won't interrupt any more meetings." He sat back down and opened his laptop, no longer paying me any attention.

My face was hot with anger, like every other time he blew up at me. But he had technically said yes, and that was all I needed. I pinned the permission slip on the fridge with a sign that said *Please sign this!* and escaped to my room.

Chapter 5

Tony Anderson: Agent-In-Training

The last time I was on a plane was when Dad was forced to take me on a business trip because he couldn't find a babysitter. I was seven at the time, and he hasn't taken me anywhere since.

The plane rattled for a second, and I looked out the window at the clouds below us. This was going to be the best summer ever.

The morning after I tried to tell him about camp, I came downstairs to an empty house with a signed permission slip. He technically didn't need to sign anything for me to join the T.S.O. and start my training. It was proof for Ms. Blanchard, so she knew I actually told him and didn't end up going to camp without parental knowledge of any kind.

The last couple months of school had been painstakingly slow. Summer couldn't have gotten here fast enough. Now, here I was.

I grabbed my bag from the overhead compartment on the plane and walked down the aisle. I was put on a plane going to Sacramento, California. California heat greeted me the second I left the airport. I stood outside where the drop off line was cluttered with waiting cars.

"Mr. Anderson?"

I jumped at the sound of my name. An airport security officer stood behind me. "Yes?" I asked, regaining my composure.

"Follow me, please." The man nodded, then turned without waiting to see if I would follow. I swallowed the nerves and excitement and followed the man. He stopped in front of a white car at the end of the curb and opened the door. "Put your hand here," he said.

The security officer pulled a tablet shaped device from the car and held it out to me. I pressed my hand against the screen. It flashed green. Awesome. A hand scanner. How did they get my handprint in their system? Ms. Blanchard. The security officer pulled it away and nodded towards the car. I ducked into the back and stared outside as the car drove off.

I couldn't believe it. I was going to be an agent. Me. It was the kind of thing my friends would have loved. The guys wouldn't care. I wanted to tell Amelia and Emily. I imagined the two of them sitting in the back of the car with me, smiling and talking about this awesome adventure.

Amelia still wasn't acting quite right when I had left. I couldn't tell if Emily noticed anything off about her or not. If only they were here with me right now. They wouldn't believe I was going to be an agent even if I could tell them.

A smile spread across my face. The Teen Spy Organization wanted me. I didn't understand why, but hey, camp was going to be a blast. It sounded much better than sitting at home while Dad spent every waking moment working, doing his best to ignore me.

The back windows in the car wouldn't roll down. There was a wall between me and the front seats, so I couldn't see the driver. In a way it was unsettling, but I told myself it didn't bother me. This was how agents traveled, right? With the utmost secrecy. About an hour passed before the car stopped. The door unlocked, and I stepped out. I was at a bus station.

A woman approached me, and I shifted my bag over my shoulder. She wore silver sunglasses and a T-shirt and jeans. Not exactly the James Bond type of look. "Tony Anderson?" she asked, looking me up and down.

"That's me," I said.

"Place your hand here, please." She held out another tablet and I did as she said. The screen flashed green just like it did at the airport. "This way."

The car backed out of the parking spot, leaving me standing beside this very normal looking woman. She led me to a line of buses. People were boarding a couple, others stepping off. She stopped in front of a bus in the middle of the fleet. "Climb aboard."

I stepped onto the bus and into the aisle, noticing about ten kids already on the bus, and took a seat in the middle of the row, right beside the window. This was not what I was expecting. Maybe the cool cars and private jets were only for trained agents. After a couple more people boarded, all ranging in age and appearance, the wheels started moving.

Chapter 6

Welcome to Cabin Eleven

The bus kept driving.

And driving.

Where were we going? I looked at the other passengers, most of them kids, and they all looked as confused as I did. Where did they all come from? Did Ms. Blanchard personally recruit them, too? There were two adults not including the bus driver, but neither of them gave us any attention. I sighed and leaned back against the seat. This had better not have been a mistake. I tried to tell the time by watching the sun but gave up after about an hour. It had to be lunchtime. My flight had left at six that morning. I should have worn a watch.

Finally, the bus screeched to a stop. My stomach flipped as I gawked out the window. I grabbed my suitcase from the overhead compartment, slung my backpack over my shoulders, and squeezed out the bus along with everyone else.

The camp was huge. In front of me was a large clearing, cabins set up all around the open space. About a mile away from every edge of the cabins, red wood trees blocked the view of anything else, enclosing the camp.

"Check in!" A man yelled. "Check in over here!"

I stepped up to a table set up in front of the bus. "Name?" he asked. The man was probably in his thirties, his face covered by the beginnings of a beard.

"Tony Anderson."

The man grabbed my arm and pressed my hand against a tablet on the table. It was just like the one that scanned my hand the last two times. A green light moved up and down on the device. "You know," I said. "A handprint can be easily faked with the right material or some residue left on that screen."

"Cabin eleven." He stared up at me, no emotion on his face. "It's on the left." The man typed something into his computer, then looked up at me with raised eyebrows. "Welcome to camp, kid."

I found cabin eleven. It looked small from the outside, was made of wood, and had a porch wrapped around the front. The air smelled so fresh, I stopped and took it all in. It was so green.

I stepped up onto the porch and yanked the door handle. The door wouldn't open. I scrunched my brow as I pulled harder.

"It's locked." Beside the door, a face was squished up against the window screen. Why would the door be locked? "You've got to use the scanner," the face said through the window.

I looked back at the door. Beside it was the same device that was back on the table where I signed in. I put my hand up to the scanner and waited for the beep. Much to my relief, the door opened.

"Welcome to cabin eleven."

I dropped my backpack next to my suitcase. The same kid who talked to me through the window stepped up to me. "The name's Ethan." I shook hands with him. His blond hair was so long it almost covered his eyes. It reminded me of a dog's fur.

"Thanks. I'm Tony."

I looked around the cabin. It was smaller than I expected. I was imagining a high-tech cabin with a flat screen TV and secret tunnels leading to the other buildings, considering this was a fancy spy agency and all that. But it was just a normal cabin. Three bunk beds were against the walls. Six lockers covered the other wall in the room. Who knew? Maybe it just looked normal.

There were three other guys in the cabin.

"First time?" one of them asked. He was lying across his bunk, a comic book in his hands.

"Yep. You?"

"This is my first time here, too. I'm Handel." He went back to his comic book.

I grabbed an empty bunk on the back wall.

"I'm Oliss," another said, his gray eyes staring at me like I was the enemy. "Second year." I nodded, making a mental note not to get on the kid's bad side. "That's Bentley." Oliss pointed to the bunk above him, where another guy sat. With two fingers to his forehead, he gave me a salute, his face as neutral as it possibly could be.

"You think this place has good food?" Ethan asked, rubbing his hands together.

"It's okay," Oliss, answered. I listened to him talk about the typical cafeteria food, healthy and satisfying, as I emptied my bags. My locker required a hand scan to open it, which made me rethink the whole "normal cabin" thing. It was awesome!

Five minutes later, a horn blew, making me jump.

26

"All campers, report to the pit for orientation," a voice said through a loudspeaker I couldn't see.

"We better go," Oliss said. "First rule of camp? Never be late."

Chapter 7

The Rock Wall and the Leather Jacket

My stomach did back flips as I stepped off the porch behind Bentley. The excitement was growing with every step. I followed my cabin mates down the walkway, gazing at the cabins we passed.

The horn sounded again. The other guys from my cabin were halfway across the field, running towards the back of the camp towards the lake. I followed behind.

This place had everything.

As I walked down the path, I read the signs identifying each building. There was a gym, multiple classrooms, and a cafeteria. The smells of our next meal seeped through the doors as I passed. My stomach grumbled. A building made of gray brick had a sign that said "Science Lab."

I followed the other campers but stopped when something else caught my eye. I could see the tip of a rock wall reaching out behind the gym. My curiosity got the better of me. Moving away from the group, I walked down the path and towards the rock wall.

It was insane. I wasn't the only teenager who left the group to explore. Two girls and a guy who was at least six feet tall stood in front of it.

"And that was before they installed the safety equipment," one of the girls said.

"What?" I stepped closer, the three teens turning to look at me.

"You haven't heard?" the girl asked.

"This is my first year. What are you talking about?" My eyes widened at the possibility of a story.

"A few years ago, a camper - she's an agent now - had a really bad accident."

I looked up at the rock wall. It was the shape of half a circle and at least four stories high. It wasn't like the rock walls you see at amusement parks. It didn't have plastic handholds. The entire thing was *real* rock. Only one side of the wall had a safety rope hanging on it. "You see the blue mat on the ground?" the girl asked.

"Yeah." I looked at the large mat sitting on top of the dirt. It had to be about two feet thick.

"They didn't used to have it. Now they even have a net that moves up and down in case someone falls during training." She moved her hands up and down to demonstrate.

"Tell him the story," the guy said. These kids had to be second years, to already know crazy stories about past campers.

The girl began to speak.

"The agent was doing her training on the wall, but she lost her grip. She wasn't harnessed either. The story says she was three quarters of the way up and fell all the way to the floor. She gashed her leg open on the way down."

"Wow," the other girl said. "Was she okay?"

"They say she hit her head pretty hard," the guy continued. "It took the rest of camp for her to recuperate, but she didn't go home. I'm told her bruises were awful and the concussion must have left a mark. But that gash on her leg still leaves a nasty scar."

The girl picked it back up. "One of the instructor tried to catch her, but he barely cushioned the fall."

I didn't say anything. Even thinking about it made my head hurt. They seriously let people do that before with no safety precautions. And these kids thought that was cool? What was I getting myself into? On the other hand, it was an awesome story. "That must have hurt," I said.

"It hurt like heck." I spun around to the new voice. She stood behind us, her hands on her hips. She wore a leather jacket, sunglasses, and fingerless gloves. Despite her dangerous appearance, there was a pull of a smile at the edge of her lips.

"That's her," one of the girls whispered. I stared.

"Get off to orientation." the girl said. Her voice was firm and demanding. "The T.S.O. doesn't accept slackers."

Wonderful. I had only been here twenty minutes, and I already broke rule one. Which one would I break next?

Chapter 8

Welcome to Camp

The pit wasn't as bad as it sounded. I was picturing something dark and ominous. I thought the pit would be a large hole, a chasm into the earth, maybe something kids would have to bungee jump off to test their bravery. Really, it was a large fire pit with a stage set up in front of the lake. All the campers were crowded as close to the stage as possible, but everyone stood in some sort of organized pattern with their cabin. I found the other guys from cabin eleven.

"Where have you been?" Handel asked.

"Sorry. Got distracted," I whispered. Oliss rolled his eyes at me.

"Attention, campers!"

I looked up at the stage. Ms. Blanchard spoke into a microphone at center stage. The entire place went silent. If I had to guess, I would have said there were about a hundred kids in all, from the ages of thirteen to seventeen.

"Welcome to the T.S.O. Training Camp."

Ten people stood behind Ms. Blanchard, but I couldn't see who they were from the glare of the sun. The director wore a navy-blue suit, her hair curled back away from her face. "My name is Ms. Blanchard. I am the director of the Teen Spy Organization's Headquarters. I'm also your camp leader.

"Today you begin your training to join the most secret underground agency in the United States. An organization that prides itself on its young agents and their work towards making the nation safer."

I listened as hard as I could. Amelia would have loved this.

"Here you will be trained to become an agent, forced to reach your limit physically and mentally. Then you will be required to expand that limit. The T.S.O. prides itself on three pillars; strength of mind, body, and soul. These are the strengths we intend to instill in you this summer."

I looked over at Bentley, who was standing next to me. He raised an eyebrow, then turned back to the director.

"For second year campers, you already know the routine," Ms. Blanchard continued. "Classes start at O-seven-thirty in the morning. Curfew is at twenty-two hundred hours. That's ten o'clock. You will be given your schedules by the supervising officers before heading to lunch. The list of rules will also be included with your schedules as well as a map of the grounds.

"Camp is the first level of training. A camper must attend two years of camp before graduating to advanced courses which are held at all T.S.O. bases across the country. At the end of the summer, all campers will participate in our annual agent-training challenge to finish off the summer. But you have to make it to the end of the summer first."

Oliss crossed his arms. Ethan stared at Ms. Blanchard like a puppy. I probably was too. A competition? It sounded important, fun. I shifted my feet as I looked back at the director.

"Before dismissing you to lunch and your first classes, I would like to introduce this year's instructors."

One by one the director called out an agent's name and one of the people standing behind her stepped up. Agent Willows oversaw the science division. She wore glasses that made her face look smaller against the sunlight. Agent P.R. was in charge of Gadgetry and Logistical Tactics. That sounded interesting. The director went further and further down the line until a person stepped up and made me do a double take.

"Agent Mills," the director said. A brown-haired girl wearing a leather jacket and fingerless gloves stepped up. "Agent Mills is our first-year Defense Tactics and second-year Combat instructor."

I stared at her. I couldn't stop thinking about what I'd heard at the rock wall. The person who survived that accident was going to teach me how to fight? Agent Mills stepped back as Ms. Blanchard called out the next name. Agent Mills. She seemed kind of scary. In a very cool way.

"And finally," The director said, drawing my attention back to her. "Agent Powell." A man stepped up on the stage. He wore a doctor's coat over a T-shirt and jeans. "Agent Powell is the head doctor on site. He will be stationed in the infirmary, which you can find near the cafeteria. Have fun campers. You are all dismissed."

Chapter 9

Review of the Schedules

An adult handed me a file as I entered the cafeteria. Everyone in my cabin received a similar looking folder.

You are all dismissed. How formal. The seriousness of this place was starting to sink in.

Between the use of military time and Ms. Blanchard's tone, my decision to come here felt like a rock in my head. Heavy. Becoming a spy sounded cool, but this was too real.

Ever since Ms. Blanchard first approached me, I wasn't entirely sure what to expect. It all seemed so out of the ordinary. A secret agent recruiter at my school, me being chosen of all people. I felt like there were other kids more qualified than I to be here. My skills were being recognized. That was a new feeling for me, and I liked it more than I wanted to admit.

Everyone filed into the cafeteria, filled their plates, and sat at their designated table. The rest of cabin eleven and myself were seated in the middle of the room. There were four large TV screens put together on the far wall. Under the screens, all the instructors sat at their own table.

The salad was fresh, and the grilled chicken was perfect. I settled in as I enjoyed my meal. Handel came to sit beside me. Oliss took a seat on the other side as the others filed in.

"What do your schedules say?" Handel asked. He spooned food into his mouth before glancing at his own schedule.

I put down my fork, taking my schedule out of my file. "O-seven-thirty to O-eight-thirty I have Logistical Tactics. O-Eight-thirty to O-nine-thirty is Gadgetry. O-Nine-thirty to O-ten-thirty is Field Operations. Then I have History."

"I have that one too!" Ethan exclaimed. He spilled rice onto his schedule as he scarfed food into his mouth.

"I have Logistical Tactics with you," Handel said. He called out the rest of his classes. "Then there's lunch."

I didn't finish reading my schedule. That could all be sorted out later. I took a bite of the chicken on my plate, and Ethan took over the conversation with what was written on his paper. "Hey, I have free time at two!"

"Me too," Handel said.

Bentley nodded. So did Oliss. I looked down at my paper. We all had the same free time. "What do you do during then?" I asked.

Oliss answered. "A lot of kids hang out in their cabins or down by the lake. There are canoes available for anyone to use. If you're smart, you'll use it as extra training time."

"Extra training time?" I asked.

"Physical combat is the most difficult thing around here for most people. Either that or the sciences for year two trainees. If you want to be an agent, you have to know how to fight. First-year campers have Defense Tactics and second years have a more advanced, offensive combat class." Bentley nodded in agreement with Oliss. "Especially if you want any chance in the agent-training games at the end of the summer, you'll train every chance you get."

"Really?" Ethan asked.

"It puts every single skill you learn here to the test."

"So," Handel started. "Do you guys know why you were recruited?"

I thought for a moment. Ms. Blanchard had never told me specifically why the T.S.O. wanted me. I guess I had the skills that an agent would need. At the time that was good enough for me to say yes to all this. I didn't know how my pranks or unclogging drains equated to secret-agent skills, and I wasn't about to admit to being a prankster before knowing these guys.

"No clue," I said, trying not to feel self-conscious. My father found all my talents mute compared to his opinions of success.

"They never tell you," Oliss said. "Everyone I've talked to, no one is ever told why they were recruited other than they have potential, at least not until they become an agent."

"Interesting," Ethan said. He stared at the empty plate in front of him.

A horn blew. Kids began leaving their tables as the sounds of dishes clanking together mixed with voices.

"You guys better get to your first class. Remember, you don't want to be late." Oliss picked up his plate. "You guys might want to read that rule sheet as soon as possible. See you all at dinner." Oliss left the table. Bentley got up and followed him.

"See you guys later," I said. I could hear my heartbeat speeding up as I opened the cafeteria doors and paused outside. I looked down at my paper. I frowned. My very first class was Defense Tactics with Agent Mills. The one with the leather jacket.

Why couldn't I start with the easy stuff, like science or Gadgetry? That sounded like a cool class. Combat was not my area of expertise. My mind drifted back to our conversation over lunch. Why was I here? What had Ms. Blanchard seen in me? Did she really think I could make a good agent, or was she trying to get another sad, lonely kid off the street before he did something he would regret?

At least I wasn't at home avoiding my father. I glanced back down at my schedule. Maybe I would even learn something in this class, learn how to fight. If I learned how to handle myself, maybe I wouldn't be so afraid of him. My father. I had never done anything important until making the decision to come here. I knew that much.

Then there was that memory again.

The voices screaming at each other, my father throwing his glass across the room. The slamming of the door as my mother left our lives for good. I didn't blame her. My father was a difficult man to live with. His anger was only outmatched by his aim. And what did I do that night? I hid on the stairs, tears falling as fear kept me frozen in place. I did nothing to help the one person that had always been there for me.

I stood up straighter, coming to a decision. I had to learn how to fight. If I was going to protect people, it would start with protecting myself. Defense Tactics was as good a place as any. The little boy in my memory was too scared to stand up, too scared to get involved, to face his father when it really mattered. I would leave this camp no longer that little boy.

I shoved the schedule into my pocket and headed down the walkway. This was going to be fun, right?

Chapter 10

Defense Tactics

In the locker room, I found my gym uniform. Black shorts and a blue T-shirt. I left my file in the locker and entered the gym.

Half the floor was matted. The back corner of the room was filled with equipment. Weights, punching bags, boxes, a rack of sticks, some extra mats, and more. Nine other people stood in the room, looking either lost, scared, or excited. Based on the nervous feeling in my gut, I was probably on the scared side. Thanks a lot, Oliss.

"Alright, listen up!"

I jerked my head to the door just in time to watch it slam shut behind Agent Mills. The ten of us formed a line on the mat as Agent Mills walked to the front of the room. Bile was stuck in my throat.

"This class isn't about beating up other people," she said. She looked overly excited in a way that made me want to run. Fight or flight? I didn't exactly have a choice.

The girl standing next to me raised an eyebrow. "Really?"

"Really." Agent Mills glared at her. She was still wearing her leather jacket and gloves. "This class is about discipline, self-control, and defending yourself."

Agent Mills stopped pacing and stood at the front of the room. She looked young compared to the other instructors who were all adults. How old was Agent Mills? Her voice was calmer when she spoke again.

"When I call out your names, say 'here.' Understood?"

The agent unfolded a paper from her pocket and started reading off names. I shifted my weight from foot to foot and tried not to make eye contact with Agent Mills. In an odd way, she kind of reminded me of Amelia. Maybe it was because she seemed so determined. Although, in a wilder sort of way.

Agent Mills continued reading. "Tony Anderson."

"Here." I stood up straighter.

"Ahh, the curious one." Agent Mills smiled at me.

"Excuse me?" The moment I said it I knew I shouldn't have.

"Don't worry." She let out a chuckle. "I don't bite. We'll turn you into an agent by the time the summer is over."

I frowned, looking down as she continued through her list.

"Alright, first things first. This class is going to be difficult. But if you want to become an agent, you have to know how to defend yourself in the field. Even office agents are trained in physical combat. In this class you will be trained how to fight to protect yourself."

I hoped she would say something along the lines that fighting isn't always necessary, combat is just for the movies, but she didn't.

"Before you can learn to flip someone or break someone's arm," Agent Mills continued, "You need to be able to physically handle it. Any questions?"

"Why would I need to break someone's arm?" one of the guys asked.

"You never know what situations you might find yourself in," she said. "You could be trapped in a penthouse where you're forced to fight your way out while protecting your team or jumping off a train while being chased by bad guys." I raised an eyebrow. "Just an example." Agent Mills shrugged. "In this class you will learn not only to fight, but to endure pain so you *can* fight."

I forced myself to swallow the lump in my throat. Wonderful.

"So, to start off, give me twenty pushups!"

Chapter 11

The One Who Caused Me Pain

Pain.

That was the only thing going through my head that I understood. My knees were ready to crumble. My arms felt like noodles. At least I wasn't bleeding or bruised. Yet. Unclogging the sink at that soup kitchen was more fun than this.

We had done planks, pushups, jumping jacks, and crunches. Just to name a few. Just about all of class time was taken up doing this. Yet somehow, I still had a separate Physical Training class.

Leather Jacket just wanted us to be "in shape" so we could start learning how to fight tomorrow. And to top off today's class, Agent Mills decided to give a demonstration on how to take down an attacker with a gun. Guess who she picked as a volunteer.

I stood at the front of the room, hundreds of possible scenarios running through my head while everyone stared at me. She mentioned breaking arms. Was she going to do that? I felt sick.

"Here." Agent Mills handed me a gun. I stared at it, my palm sweaty. What was I supposed to do with this? "It's fake," she said.

"Right." I took the gun from her and followed her instructions; place the gun in the middle of her back.

I let the rubber end of the gun rest between her shoulder blades. This was not going to end well, was it?

"Many people think guns are the answer," Agent Mills started. "A gun is a good weapon, but when in the wrong hands they are violent and dangerous. I'll tell you right now. I don't like guns. If you are hit with a fatal shot, you're an agent down. Not only does this harm you and possibly your comrades in the field, but it leaves questions. If your parents find out you've been shot, there is no way you're going back to the agency, not for a while. So, one of the first things we'll learn is to disarm your attacker. That's important in making it out of a fight alive. The second key is knowing how to overpower them."

Before I could say anything else, Agent Mills turned on me. She spun around, hooking her arm around mine. She grabbed the gun, jerked it to face me just as her elbow rammed into my nose. The rubber gun was forced from my fingers. Before I could regain my stance, her boot connected with my stomach, knocking me backwards onto the ground.

I groaned. Agent Mills smirked.

"That is how you disarm someone from behind. We'll work on disarming tomorrow with guns as well as knives. We'll also learn about pressure points."

I got to my feet, clenching my stomach. My nose was burning, but it wasn't bleeding. Why was this happening to me? I was starting to think becoming an agent was a mistake. And I hadn't even been here a whole day. This girl's ability to take me down so quickly was both impressive and intimidating.

"You are dismissed."

I pulled myself off the mat and followed the others to the door.

"Anderson!" I froze. What did I do wrong?

"Yes?" I walked up to Agent Mills, struggling to right myself without holding my stomach. "Ma'am?"

"Thank you for assisting me," she said. "And don't call me Ma'am."

"No problem." I tried to smile but my face hurt too much, my nose still burning. It probably looked more like a grimace.

"Where are you from?" she asked.

"California. Do I get to ask you a question?" I was hoping the answer wasn't another kick in the ribs.

"You're funny. What part of California?" As she asked the question her brows furrowed, and her tough-guy act didn't look so intimidating.

"Glayfield," I said, a little more at ease.

"Really?" Agent Mills smiled to herself. She knew something I didn't. It was unnerving. "Alright, what's your question?"

I stood up straighter. I was not expecting her to actually let me ask her anything. "First of all, ow." She smirked. I tried to come up with something to ask her, just to prove I wasn't chicken. "Why do you wear a leather jacket?" I asked.

Agent Mills pondered the question for a moment, a gentle smile spreading across her face. "You are a curious one, aren't you?" She faced me. "I've always worn it, ever since I became an agent. And I just got a new one!" She looked down at the sleeves and pulled on the zipper, admiring her own attire. "This one is bulletproof and fireproof." She looked proud of it.

"Why?" I asked.

"Let's just say after my last case, I needed some upgrades." I nodded, not quite sure what she meant. "You

43

can go now. Just remember, curiosity can be dangerous, and some people won't like it as much as I do. This job is a lot harder than you think. I'll see you tomorrow for class."

I nodded warily. Curiosity can be dangerous? I didn't know what I was supposed to think about that.

Chapter 12

To Prank or Not to Prank

I grabbed my dinner tray and met my cabin mates at the table. Spaghetti and meatballs, nothing sounded better after getting my butt kicked by a girl. I hadn't even been at camp for a day, and I was exhausted. The guys shared about their first class between full mouths of noodles.

"What did you think of combat?" Oliss asked.

I turned to Ethan, who had a bruise forming on his temple. "Did that happen in class?" I asked, ignoring his question.

Ethan laughed nervously. "No. During free time I was exploring and ran into a pole on the volleyball courts."

"Seriously?" Handel asked.

"I wasn't paying attention!"

"What about combat, Tony?" Oliss asked again.

"I didn't realize how hard it would be," I said.

"It's hard, yes," Oliss said. "But it will be one of your most crucial classes. A field agent needs to know how to fight."

I found myself glancing around the room and spotting Agent Mills walking towards the instructors' table.

"Maybe all of us aren't destined to be field agents," Handel said.

Oliss shrugged, a quiet joke spreading across his lips. "That's true. Only the best are given that position." He swirled spaghetti onto his fork and shoved it in his mouth. "Still, you've got to do your best in all your classes if you want to make it out of here unscathed."

What was his deal? I frowned at Oliss. Why was he so uptight, so pushy? Sure, being a field agent was where the action was, but that didn't mean it was the only valuable job. Right?

"So, do you people have any secret traditions around here like other camps do?" Ethan asked. He leaned closer to the table like the question itself was a secret.

"What do you mean?" Oliss asked. Bentley raised an eyebrow at him.

"You know," Ethan said. "Like prank wars or secret challenges between cabins. When I was younger, I went to this summer camp where all the cabins had secret wars after lights out for fun."

A dozen ideas burned in my mind. I was the prank master, wasn't I?

Oliss shook his head seriously. "Absolutely not," he said. "This place isn't a game, okay? People here are expected to become professional secret agents. There isn't any time for goofing off or pranking each other just for a laugh. This is serious business. If someone did that here, they would probably get kicked out."

I snickered. If someone was dumb enough to try something and got caught, that was their own fault. Agents-in-training pulling prank wars sounded like a great idea. A way to test your skills.

"What's so funny, Anderson?" Oliss growled at me.

46

"Nothing," I said.

Oliss shook his head in disgust and went back to his food. Handel and Ethan looked at me, and I smiled out of the corner of my mouth. How could I possibly go to any type of camp and not mess around a little? It was what I was good at, which caught Ms. Blanchard's attention in the first place.

That night in the cabin, Handel threw himself on his bunk and buried his face in a comic book. Once Oliss and Bentley left for the showers, Ethan climbed down from his bed.

"Well?" Ethan asked, his eyes brimming with curiosity.

"Well, what?"

"Come on, man," he said. "We saw your look. You've got some tricks up your sleeve. Don't hold out on us." He leaned against the bedpost and crossed his arms. Handel propped himself up to look at us.

I shoved my shoes under the bed and smiled. "Back home I was like the king of pranks. My friend Amelia, she was the only one who always caught on. And our other friend, Emily, has always been the perfect target. Very gullible."

Ethan smiled. "So, what do you have in mind? Everyone around here is so hardheaded."

"You don't think what Oliss said is true?" Handel asked.

I frowned. "He's probably right, but he's as hardheaded as anyone else around here. Probably even more."

"Well, do you have a plan or not?" Ethan asked.

"Oh, I have a few ideas," I said. "The goal here is picking the right target. Someone that wouldn't snitch if they found out it was us. And we have to find a prank that isn't too harmful. You have to start out small, test the tension in the rope before you step on it, if you know what I mean."

Handel nodded thoughtfully. "So, you think we could pull something off?" he asked. Handel paused, his eyes drifting before he spoke again. "You have to know; I can't get caught doing something wrong. I've been there. No illegal shenanigans, or I don't know about it."

"We can definitely pull something like that," I said, raising an eyebrow at him. I brushed away his comment. "I say let's learn our way around here a little, give it another day or so to test the playing field before we make any decisions."

Ethan nodded eagerly. I realized what I was signing up for, and the eagerness of the two was not completely positive. If I was going to cause some mayhem, which was sounding more intriguing by the minute, I needed a crew that was fully onboard.

"Here's the thing," I said. "If you're in, you're in. No backing out, and no snitching. Deal?"

"Deal," they said in unison.

Chapter 13

Class is in Session

Agent P.R. stood behind a table filled with the most intricate pieces of technology I had ever seen. They were all so different and unique, I couldn't tell you what any of them did just by looking at them. The pile of pens on the table caught my attention. What did those do? Maybe I could learn something in this class we could use for our prank.

"Alrighty," Agent P.R. started after taking attendance. "First I want to show you guys a very simple but useful tool."

I sat in my seat, feet tapping against the floor as I waited for him to continue.

He picked up a pair of glasses from the end of the table. "This is the latest pair of night vision goggles we've designed." They looked like bulky sunglasses. The frame was black, with the rim extending from the lenses to touch the wearer's face. Other than that, they looked like normal sunglasses. "This tool is extremely useful when you're working at night. You don't want to become blind just because of the sun disappearing."

And that's how class continued.

Turns out, the twenty pens sitting on the table each did something different. One was a grappling hook, another a listening and recording device. One pen wrote with acid.

After Agent P.R. finished explaining each device on the table, he took the night vision goggles and passed them around, each of us trying them on. They were the coolest thing I had ever seen. When they made it to my table, I slid the glasses on. They blocked out all light, feeling snug around my ears. Through them I could see everything in a green filter with perfect definition.

This was the cool part of being a spy, and it didn't involve any combat to learn how these gadgets worked. Maybe camp would be more exciting than Oliss wanted us to believe.

I was not prepared for a history class to be interesting. Ms. Blanchard stood in front of the class, Dr. Powell beside her. "Take a seat, everyone!" she called as we filed into the room. I sat at a desk beside Ethan, curious about how this class would go.

"For those of you who haven't met me yet, my name is Ms. Blanchard. I'm Director of Headquarters and oversee all recruitment and training. This is Agent Powell."

"Dr. Powell," he cut in, smiling at the class.

"I will be your main instructor for this course, but if something is ever to come up, Dr. Powell will be taking over." She paced across the room, hands folded behind her back. "Now. Welcome to the Teen Spy Organization. As an agent-in-training, it's important for you to know and understand our history and our mission. Without that, there would be no T.S.O."

Ms. Blanchard pulled up a PowerPoint. "Take notes, because there will be a test." I pulled out a notebook. Of course there would be a test. The first slide caught my attention though, and the boringness of the class evaporated.

There was a black and white picture of a group of kids beside a building, or should I say, what was left of it. Smoke billowed out of the windows and the remaining ruble. There was one girl in the front who looked an awful lot like Ms. Blanchard. "World War II ended in 1945," Ms. Blanchard continued. She was too young to be the same person in the photo. She had to be. "For the sake of this class, I will not cover the details of the war. You should know that already. What's important are these kids right here."

Dr. Powell picked up. "These kids were not allowed to fight in the war. It was illegal to join the military under the age of seventeen. These kids here didn't accept that. They created their own group here in the states, fighting crime in their neighborhoods under the cover of night. This included solving robberies and stopping some domestic violence, putting out fires and quietly helping with the war effort. Nothing that would get them noticed. They would call in tips to the police and leave criminals for the cops to pick up."

"Like superheroes," Ethan said.

"Yes, like superheroes." Ms. Blanchard smiled. "Other kids slowly joined, and they became a secret club. They called themselves the Teenage Agents. Nobody really knew the truth about their existence. This was how the Teen Spy Organization began.

"When these original kids became adults, they wanted to keep their mission going. They believed they could make a difference. Some of them left, joined the military, got jobs, a couple went into politics. They continued to recruit more kids, but as time went on it got harder and harder to keep up with their mission.

"This woman here," Ms. Blanchard pointed to the girl in the photo that looked like her. "Her name is Sylvia. She is my grandmother. When I was thirteen, she introduced me to the secret group of teenagers that were fighting to keep our city safe."

Dr. Powell pointed to a girl standing next to Sylvia. "This is my grandmother. I was also introduced to the Teenage Agents, and together Ms. Blanchard and myself became big parts of this underground force."

A silence washed over us as we took in this information. I stared at the teenagers in the photo, amazed at what they started. This was real.

Ms. Blanchard continued her lecture. "The problem was that we were not official, and we could not be official because we were minors. We lacked organization and funding.

"After a lot of arguments, meetings, and compromises, we created a plan of action. We set up an idea for a secret agency, how it would be run, who would be in charge, and what we would be working towards. Then we found investors. There were still original members of the Teenage Agents out there, as I said holding different official positions, or living in retirement. None of them are pictured here, and for their protection they will not be named."

Ms. Blanchard looked at the photo on the slide, then back to us. "We reached out to these people, explained to them what we wanted to do with their original group, and we asked for funding. These original Teenage Agents and their businesses, legacies, and children are the reasons you're here. Without any of them, there would be no Teen Spy Organization.

Chapter 14

Phone Calls in the Woods

My body felt permanently sore from Defense Tactics class and Physical Training by the end of the week, but it was worth it. I appreciated what I was learning. Gadgetry class was my favorite, with Logistical Tactics coming in second. We spent the first class in Logistical Tactics talking about what makes a good team, learning to trust each other, and knowing how to work together in the field.

History was intriguing. The history of the T.S.O. still amazed me when I thought about it throughout the day. We were going to go into more detail about the past, about the Teenage Agents. We would start learning how the T.S.O. functions today as class went on.

A routine had started to form. I had managed to avoid Agent Mills, other than her class. She hadn't bothered me anymore, but I caught her looking at me from time to time. A guilty feeling started forming deep in my stomach. But what did I have to be guilty about? I didn't do anything wrong. Yet. How would she react if she was the target of a prank? Part of me really wanted to find out.

PT had wiped me out today, and it was time for dinner. I turned the corner around the gym and entered the clearing. Smells from the cafeteria wafted through the front doors as I got closer. Something savory was cooking and calling my name.

"She seems pretty normal so far," a voice said.

I froze a few yards from the cafeteria. It was Agent Mills, speaking in a hushed voice.

I looked around, the closest building being a classroom next to the cafeteria. I crept back to the side of the building, out of sight. Her voice was coming from behind the cabin. I wanted to peak but forced myself to stay glued to the wall. Getting caught was not an option. Was this what being a spy felt like?

"Okay, Tanner. I'll keep an eye out. Let me know if you hear anything else."

There was no answer. Was she on the phone?

A moment passed. I watched Agent Mills disappear around the other side of the building. I peeked around the other side of the cabin in time to see her step into the cafeteria. My heartbeat slowed once the cafeteria doors closed behind her. Who was Tanner? Who was she talking about?

I stared at the lawn, thoughts flying through my head. Whether the phone call was business or personal, it had to be something important. A smile crossed my lips.

Maybe, just maybe I could have some fun with pranks, and practice my spy techniques at the same time.

Chapter 15

Making Smoke Bombs

Agent Mill's secret phone call made me toss and turn all night. By the time the sun was up, a plan was forming in my mind. It was the second week of classes, and I was excited. I listened hard in class, but I spent every spare moment working out the details. It was time to cause a little trouble around here.

"I've got it!" I burst through the cabin to find Bentley staring at me. "Where is everyone?"

He shrugged his shoulders and turned back to the paper in his hand. I threw the door open and dashed across the giant lawn.

There they were. Handel and Ethan hauled a canoe towards the lake.

"Guys!" Their heads turned in my direction. They dropped the canoe and waited for me to catch up. "Guys, I got it!" My breath was coming out choppy.

"Got what?" Handel asked.

"What we're going to do," I said. "Our first target." Ethan smiled like a puppy and moved to put the canoe back.

"Actually," I said, "let's talk out there." I pointed to the lake. "Less ears."

When we had the canoe out on the water, away from the shore and prying eyes of agents-in-training, we put down the oars.

"So?" Ethan asked.

"Agent Mills."

They stared at me. After a long moment, Handel spoke up. "You're joking, right?"

"Think about it," I said. "I've been watching her all week."

"More like avoiding her," Handel mumbled.

I glared at him. "She's a hardheaded person that doesn't like to be made fun of. No matter what we do, she won't tell anybody. She would be too embarrassed. I have a feeling she might even think it funny enough to just let it go. She can't get us into trouble, trust me."

"How are you so sure about that?" Handel asked.

"Yeah, didn't she kick you in the ribs?" Ethan made a face. He just had to bring that up, didn't he?

I remembered the night before, when I caught Agent Mills having a secret phone call. My mind drifted to the countless memories of my father on the phone, walking through the house, ignoring me.

"Tony?"

I looked up from the oar in my hand and met their eyes. "Trust me, guys. It will be fun."

Handel nodded. "Nothing illegal?" he asked.

"Of course not," I said. "But just so we're clear, are you okay? What is it with all the illegal stuff?"

Handel shook his head. "It's nothing."

"When my sister grows up," Ethan said, "there is no way I'm letting her come here."

"How old is your sister?" Handel asked.

"Three. But she gets into all sorts of trouble at home. Somehow, it's always my fault. Anyway, this place is way too much fun for someone like her."

I didn't know how to take that comment, so I let it go.

"Anyway," I said, directing the conversation back to the moment. "Here's what we're going to do."

It was simple, and maybe a risky start, but it would have phenomenal results. I had to test the waters, get our feet wet and see how Agent Mills reacted. That was the first rule of pranking. Make sure you can predict the outcome before doing something unpredictable. Otherwise, you would end up in detention with people who have no sense of humor.

We put the canoe back in its rack and went to work. I sent Ethan to the kitchen for some sugar, baking soda, and a roll of paper towels. Handel refused to go anywhere he wasn't allowed, so I made my way to the maintenance shed near the infirmary. It was unlocked. I opened the door and peeked inside. One of the groundskeepers stared at me with a bottle of fertilizer in his hand.

I stood up straight, looking right at him. "Agent Willows says she has a question about a chemical agent she needs for a class. I can't remember what she said it's called."

The man sighed, put his fertilizer on a shelf, and shuffled out. "Why can't she just get it herself," he mumbled. I smiled and ducked inside, closing the door behind me.

I was looking for a chemical that wasn't common. The T.S.O. had to have it though, right? I scanned the shelves looking for the right bottle. The maintenance shed was the only place that it would be reasonable to find. There it was, sitting on the bottom shelf next to the weed killer. It was a chemical commonly used to break down stumps after cutting trees called Saltpeter, or Potassium Nitrate. I learned about it when my dad hired a gardening crew to take down some trees in our backyard so he could install a patio to impress his business associates. Mom had always taught me to be careful around chemicals, to know how to use them.

I grabbed the entire bottle and shoved it in my backpack. After Gadgetry class earlier that day, I had asked Agent P.R. if I could use the classroom to practice using the gadgets and study. He obviously thought I was telling the truth, and liked me, because he said yes. I headed over to the classroom. Handel was already inside.

"Remind me again what that's for," he said.

"We're making a smoke bomb," I said, setting the bottle on a desk. "This chemical will release oxygen, helping make the smoke, without causing a fire. Hopefully."

"So, I'm assuming you've done this before."

"Absolutely," I said.

I've done it once. Amelia and I set them off years ago at Emily's birthday party as a trick.

Everything else I needed would be in this classroom, in the mini kitchen and the storage room in the back. With Handel's help, we found some duct tape, a regular pen, cotton balls, powdered dye, matches, and some paper clips. Agent P.R. explained to me that they keep all the craft supplies and party supplies here. You never knew what you would need on the job.

"I got the stuff!" Ethan shouted as he barged into the classroom.

"Perfect. Let's get to work."

We made two colored smoke bombs. Both of them were purple because it was the only colored dye we could find. We made our concoction, cut the paper towel tube in half to make two, and set up a ring pull ignition using the paperclips and matches for both of them. My plan was to only ignite one bomb. The other would be saved for later or used in case the first backfired.

"This is going to be awesome!" Ethan and I finished wrapping our little smoke grenades in duct tape while Handel insisted on starting to clean up.

"And how are we going to pull this off without getting caught?" Handel asked.

"That's the tricky part," I said. "I asked around earlier. Agent Mills is always in the gym no later than six every morning. She works out, then she showers. We'll have to get in there before her and find a hiding place. The supply closet is big enough for all three of us to squeeze in. Because these have rings to activate, all we have to do is pull the tab and throw them in the gym. Like a grenade."

"And they won't light everything on fire?" Handel asked.

"No. I promise."

"They'll light Agent Mills' attitude on fire," Ethan smiled.

I chuckled. "That's the whole idea. She'll get angry, but I think she has enough of a sense of humor to take it as it is. A prank."

"You better be right," Handel said. "Or we're all going to be in trouble."

We woke up before the sun the next day and got straight to work. I threw on a pair of sweatpants and pulled my arms through a sweatshirt, shoving Ethan and Handel through the door as quietly as possible. We snuck into the gym from the back door to the lockers and hid in the supply closet.

"Are we sure she's coming?" Ethan whispered. He and Handel crouched on the floor behind me. We were there for fifteen minutes. It was getting stuffy.

"She'll be here," I said. I peeked out the door, peering into the hallway. No one was there. "She has to be."

A few more minutes passed before old rock music caught my attention.

"That's her," Handel said. I nodded to him, the muffled music exciting me. She was here.

"Anyone want to do the honors?" I whispered into the darkness.

"This was your idea," Ethan said. "It's all yours."

I nodded even though they couldn't fully see me and slipped through the door. Tiptoeing through the locker room to the gym, I held my breath. No going back. The music got louder as I reached the door to the gym. My fingers itched as I gripped the grenade. One more step, and I would be touching the door.

The music stopped.

I froze.

My back hit the wall beside the door. I shut my eyes, willing myself to be as flat as possible.

"Hello?" Agent Mills' voice was firm but not loud. Had she seen me? I didn't move. There were no footsteps coming in my direction. "Agent Z."

She was on the phone. Another phone call. I listened, inching closer to the door. "So, you're sure? We can trust him?" There was a pause, someone talking on the other line I couldn't hear.

"When the time is right, I'll tell him…No, that sorry excuse for an agent isn't here. Have you found out anything else?" A pause. "Well, keep an eye out. Ms. Blanchard has been quiet, and my partner is on to something, but we still don't know what's really going on. He said something about an alliance between Agent Darwin and someone else. He's still trying to figure out who. Well, thanks for calling. I'll let you know when I tell him."

The silence that followed made me anxious. The music kicked back on. I let myself breathe, my grip on the smoke bomb eased.

Ethan peeked his head out from down the hallway. I glanced at him, then at the door. Ethan gestured to me, raising his eyebrows. I could hear Agent Mills' feet moving across the mat before the music got louder and drowned out her sound. It was loud enough. I met his gaze, nodded. I stared at the smoke grenade in my hand, smiled at the ingeniousness of it, and pulled the ring.

There was a spark as the striker ignited the matches, the purple smoke slowly spewing out of the top. I crouched lower, pushing the door open just enough. Agent Mills was going through some sort of routine, her back to the door. I chucked the smoke bomb into the gym and bolted down the hallway, almost running into Ethan. Purple smoke floated out of the doorway as it swung closed. I turned the corner, Ethan on my heels, and ran through the lockers. Handel stood by the back door, waiting for us. We burst through the door and ran straight for the woods, for cover away from the gym and what just might be a furious Defense Tactics Instructor.

Chapter 16

Partners in Crime and Cases

Nobody saw Agent Mills at breakfast. I imagined her brown hair tinged with purple, her jacket stained, her face a mix of purple smoke and red fury. Every time Ethan and Handel looked at each other or at me, they smiled. The anticipation of the aftermath kept me on the edge of my seat.

In Logistical Tactics, I put the thoughts of the morning aside as best I could. Agent X, our Field Operations instructor, stood in the front of the class with Agent P.R.

"Okay class, we have something fun happening this week," Agent X announced. I perked up. "We have entered the second week at camp. To celebrate, we are going to have a drill this weekend."

"What are we doing?" a girl in front of me asked.

"You are all going to go on a retrieval mission. Can anyone tell me what that is?" My hand shot up. "Anderson?"

"A retrieval mission is a case where an agent is assigned to find and or retrieve a person or object."

"Correct."

I glanced at Handel to see if he reacted, glad I remembered our previous lesson. We learned about everything from research cases, security, these retrieval missions, and even talked about more serious cases with actual bad guys and crimes to solve. A retrieval mission could be very easy, or something extremely difficult.

"You will each be put into teams of two, six teams in total," Agent P.R. said. "Tomorrow, I will give you your mission file. This is a file with all the information we have or that you need in order to carry out an assignment. This weekend, you will all carry out your mission. You cannot get caught. There will be second-year agents and instructors aware of this drill who will do anything they can to stop you. Do not let them. You have until Sunday after dinner to bring me your findings and close your case. If you do not complete your mission on time, you fail. This is to test not only your knowledge about what we've learned in this class so far, but also your field skills. This is credit for my class and your Field Operations class. Everyone understand?"

There was a disjointed chorus of "understood."

"This does not always happen in the field, but for the sake of your first drill, you will be allowed to choose your partners. Make sure you pick before you leave this room and inform me of your decision." Agent P.R. paused for a moment as students murmured amongst each other. "Tomorrow I will be assigning cases. If there aren't any questions, class is dismissed."

Handel and I locked eyes and nodded in agreement.

"What do you think our mission will be?" Handel asked.

I shrugged. "Don't know. It could be anything."

He stopped walking when I arrived at my next class.

"So, do you have anything else planned?" There was a tone of caution in his voice.

"Handel!" I turned on him. He jumped at my movement.

"What?"

"We don't talk about that in public. Ever!" I whisper shouted at him, glanced around to see if anyone was watching. "That's how you get caught."

"Right." He whispered it under his breath, nodding. "But you have to have something planned."

"Rule number two. Never strike again without knowing the results of the first attack. Not with pranks. We'll see what happens after class later. Then we make our next plan."

He nodded slowly. "Where did you get that phrase?"

I shrugged. "Video games. I think."

"I'll see you at lunch." Handel turned and headed down the field. He paused and looked back at me, a wary look on his face. "Right before your Defense class."

A small part of me prayed I would make it that far. After all, Agent Mills wasn't someone who let her target get away. She seemed like the hit first, ask questions later type of spy.

In history class, we learned about the different levels in the Teen Spy Organization. Sitting through class I let the information envelop me, a good distraction from the smoke bomb and the excitement it was sure to bring. There were six levels within the T.S.O. Each level consisted of different positions with agents at different skill levels. I copied them down from the board as Ms. Blanchard spoke.

"You are level 0," Ms. Blanchard said. Okay, there are really seven levels. "Your position in the T.S.O. is called Agent-in-Training. When you complete your two years at summer camp, you become a Level 1 agent. These are agents undergoing advanced training. You will be a level one agent for up to a year after you finish camp. During this time, you work with a mentor, learning the job in the field.

"Then there is Level 2. Level 2 agents have completed all of their training. You may be assigned a partner to work with. There are field positions and office positions based on your talents and preferences."

Ms. Blanchard continued through her slides as I made notes. Would I be a field agent or an office agent in the future? It felt like such a long way away.

"Level 3 agents have been working for the T.S.O. at least two years after completing their training. These are agents that have completed multiple cases if they hold a field agent position. Office agents in Level 3 cover more information sensitive positions.

"Level 4 agents are T.S.O. agents that have been approved to mentor or train. Whether that be as a camp instructor, a mentor in the field, or a mentor for new agents working on a base, these are agents who have completed the requirements to pass on their knowledge and skills."

I paused and read that over in my notes. So that would make Agent Mills a Level 4 agent.

"You become a Level 5 agent when you turn twenty. When you are no longer a teenager, your jobs will change. When you turn eighteen, you can begin making decisions about whether you want to continue working for the T.S.O. or not, because as an adult we cannot allow you to work in the field. Those who want to continue field work are often transferred to a legitimate organization, like the FBI or CIA. Others choose to enter the police academy, military, and so forth. Don't worry, we have our connections to make sure you succeed and have the proper experience for any position. If an agent chooses to continue with the T.S.O. they can take on office positions if they don't hold one already. There are plenty of positions that work behind the scenes of the T.S.O., and most of these are left in the hands of our adult agents. These include mission analysis, management, education, and more."

It hadn't occurred to me what would happen when teenagers became adults in the T.S.O. They were the *Teen*

Spy Organization after all. What would I want to do after I turn twenty? I shook my head. I was getting ahead of myself.

"The last level, Level 6, is only the Board of Directors and a few other HR positions," Ms. Blanchard continued. "In the T.S.O. we have five regional directors. There is no one in charge of the Teen Spy Organization. We have five bases across the country. Four of our directors, including myself, have connections to the original Teenage Agents. Together, the five directors oversee the T.S.O. We make decisions as a group regarding our cases, agents, and the direction of our organization."

I finished scribbling notes down as Ms. Blanchard paused. "Any questions?"

Chapter 17

What is my Weakness?

There is one thing every good criminal and spy knows. If you act like you know something you shouldn't, if you look guilty, that's it. No win. Everyone will be able to tell you're lying. The key to passing suspicion is confidence and attitude. If you look like nothing's wrong, people will be none the wiser. Apparently, Agent Mills knew this tactic.

Agent Mills, a Level 4 agent, stood with her hands on her hips at the top of the steps. No one was allowed inside the gym. People crowded around on the grass while she waited for everyone to show up. I was in the middle of the small crowd. She never looked at me directly, so that was a good sign. I studied her. Her jacket was clean, her boots were untarnished. How did she clean up so fast? Even a quick shower couldn't have removed the purple from her leather wardrobe. Did the smoke bomb backfire? It couldn't have. I watched it go off before I threw it.

"Alright, listen up!" Agent Mills narrowed her eyes at us, moving from one student to the next. "What is a field agent's greatest skill?" she asked. People murmured to each other, but none volunteered. "No one? Okay then. Anderson!"

I met her eyes. *Don't show anything*, I told myself. "Umm, smarts?" I asked.

"Not quite." Agent Mills lingered on me for a moment, then paced back and forth as she continued. "Although brains are important, knowing everything won't help you in the face of danger. What happens if you get caught by surprise? What do you do when you don't know who the enemy is?"

For a moment I felt like she was targeting me. Did this have something to do with my prank? But there was no way for her to connect the smoke bomb to me. She stopped and faced us, making eye contact with me again. It was like she was looking into my soul.

"The most important skill is the ability to think ahead. If you know what is happening next, have an idea of when your enemy is going to strike, you can better protect yourself and others."

Agent Mills paused. She gestured with her hand as she stopped pacing. "Here's an example," she said. "Let's say your assignment takes you into an office building. You have no gadgets with you, and your attacker is approaching. What should you be thinking about?"

"Their weaknesses?" someone asked.

Agent Mills nodded. "Yes, that's a good start. But what if you don't know their weaknesses? What if yours are more obvious? You need to be thinking about how to protect yourself and whatever your mission is. If you're on a retrieval mission, you don't want to let your prize get away. Think about what is around you that you can use to overpower your attacker. Anyone have any ideas?" I realized where she was going and raised my hand. "Anderson."

"If you're in an office, there are a lot of tools at your disposal. Throw a chair at someone, a stapler. Use an overturned desk as a barrier like in the movies. Make the fight easier on yourself, not harder."

"Right." She nodded, but didn't smile. "Think about the fight, envision it in your mind to predict what you will have to do. Don't get yourself into a situation you can't get out of. Everyone understand that?" People nodded. "Good, now follow me."

"Where are we going?" someone asked. I cringed. That was the wrong question. Agent Mills looked irritated as she glanced over her shoulder. She tugged at her fingerless gloves and kept walking.

"The gym is being cleaned right now, so we're going on a field trip," Agent Mills said.

We kept walking until we got to a sleeping cabin. We crowded onto the porch as Agent Mills turned to face us. "This room is empty, not being used by any campers right now, but furnished for your benefit. Two at a time, you will practice thinking ahead of your enemy, using this space and everything in it to your advantage. The first person to get out of the cabin wins. Who wants to go first?"

I waited outside as a couple of groups went before me. When it was my turn, I stepped inside with another guy from the class named Jackson. He was about my height, but bulkier. I hadn't once seen him struggle in Agent Mills' class. I had to think ahead.

I took a moment to scan my surroundings. It was just like my cabin, the bunk beds, the lockers. When the door closed, we gave each other an awkward smile.

"Now!" Agent Mills shouted from outside.

Before I could move, Jackson charged me. I stepped backwards, failing to move out of his way. In less time than I could blink, I rolled onto a bottom bunk, Jackson hitting his head on the rim. *Use my surroundings,* I thought.

Jackson stepped back, then charged again, leaning down to grab me. I shifted my weight and thrust my feet out, hitting him in the shoulder and the jaw. He stumbled backward. I climbed off the bed and looked around. How could I overpower a guy stronger than me? Out of nowhere, my opponent's boot collided with my forearm, sending me to the ground. I needed to focus. I could see where the whole weakness thing came in. I had to outsmart him.

Groaning, I rolled over onto my stomach, pulling my arms underneath me. I lifted my head to look at Jackson, but my eyes stopped on something else instead. A pair of combat boots sat under the bed. I grabbed one, leaned onto my shoulder, and threw it at him. It hit Jackson on the head.

As I pushed myself off the ground, I pulled a sheet off the bed and bolted for the door.

Jackson came up behind me, and I couldn't turn in time to move out of his way. He grabbed my shirt and turned me around. "What's the blanket for?" he asked in a voice way too casual for the occasion.

"Not sure yet."

As he tried to throw a punch, I stepped on the bottom bunk and jumped, holding myself against the ladder. Within a second, I wrapped the blanket around him as he stumbled forward, jumped off the ladder and pulled him back with me. Maybe I could choke him out.

Something hard hit me on the side of the head. Jackson had grabbed a book from the bed. I hadn't seen it before.

My hold on the blanket slipped. Jackson grabbed the blanket, turned around, and twisted me inside it. I reached for something, anything around me I could hit him back with, but there was nothing there. I swept my leg out from under me but missed Jackson entirely. The sheet was wrapped around my legs and my torso, forcing one arm to stay pressed by my side, unable to move. I lifted my free arm to punch him, but Jackson caught it. He twisted my arm behind me, grabbed the end of the sheet, and tied it around my wrist. I was stuck.

"Sorry, Tony." Jackson smiled triumphantly, then opened the door.

I rolled my eyes and sighed. How was I supposed to be an agent if I couldn't fight? I stared at the floor, my eyes stopping on the boot I threw at Jackson. The leather was laced with purple dust.

Chapter 18

Cigarettes

Did Agent Mills know what I did? Why was the boot here? She was obviously wearing a different pair than the one she had on that morning. I looked out the door, where Agent Mills was talking to Jackson. She smiled at me, and I couldn't tell if it was humor or pity that was painted on her face. "Go untie Anderson," she said.

The following day, everything was fine except my pride. We had received our case files earlier during class for our retrieval missions.

"Okay, what do we have?" Handel asked, opening the file in the grass in front of him. We were near the tree line behind the cabins, away from prying eyes. I scanned the file, making sense of all the information. Relief eased my nerves that he hadn't mentioned the smoke bomb. I pictured Agent Mills' now purple boots as I opened the folder.

"It's a retrieval mission," I said, refocusing my thoughts. "We're supposed to find and retrieve a flash drive. Enemy is Dr. Powell." I paused. Dr. Powell as an enemy?

"The drive was last seen in his possession and is presumed to be hidden in his bunk."

"That's the infirmary, right?"

I nodded. "No known accomplices…" I skimmed through the rest of the file. "Wow, they really went all out on this thing." There was a head shot of Dr. Powell and a description of the flash drive; small, black, ordinary.

"Do we know what's on the flash drive?" Handel asked, reading the papers himself.

"Doesn't say. I'm guessing nothing important since it's just a drill. I don't think they would share that type of information with us on a real job unless it was crucial to succeeding anyway."

Handel nodded. I read everything over again. "Anything else planned yet?" Handel asked, breaking the silence.

I looked at him. "Are you seriously that anxious to get into trouble?"

"No." He scoffed. "I just want to make sure *you* don't get into trouble. One prank was enough, and we should keep it that way."

"Don't be such a baby," I said. "Focus on the mission."

"I'm serious." His eyes seemed darker, his tone deepening with something I didn't recognize. It was like he was scolding me. I sighed, putting down the file.

"Handel, why does it bother you so much?"

He sighed. "How were you recruited?" he asked.

"Well, I pulled a prank on my friend at school and my teacher pulled me into her office. She said she could get me into trouble, or I could become a secret agent, use my skills for good." The memory flashed in my mind like it had happened yesterday.

"Exactly. Do you know why I'm here?" Handel asked. I shook my head. "Because I was a thief, Tony. My parents aren't the best role models, okay? I started hanging out with the wrong people and getting into things I shouldn't have." He glared at me as he talked so I kept my mouth shut.

"I broke into a drug store one night. My mom forced me to and said she needed more cigarettes. I was in and out of that locked building without tripping a single alarm. Easy job. I thought I was clear when this guy across the street saw me. I thought he was going to turn me in. Instead, he told me about the T.S.O. He told me I could use my skills for something important instead of ruining my life and feeling like trash. Said I could help other people instead of hurting them. That's why I joined the T.S.O. And that's why I don't want you getting into trouble."

I stared at Handel. He was a thief. His face took on a dark expression, an emotion I couldn't quite name. Misery, maybe?

"I know firsthand what it does to a person," he said. "I'll admit, I was excited that first time. I like the rush of secrecy, but I can't get addicted to the mystery in the wrong way. I don't want you to either, Tony. And Ethan looks up to you for some reason, so you shouldn't encourage a good kid to do the wrong thing."

I never thought about it like that. I looked at the file in the grass. Pranks weren't crimes. They were silly jokes, all I really had going for me. I thought they were. Handel's story made my stomach hurt, and I didn't like it. Were they recruiting us just so we didn't go down the wrong path?

"Come on," Handel said. "We have to plan out this mission."

Chapter 19

The Retrieval Mission

Handel sat on his bunk, his eyes glued to a comic book. The way he acted made more sense now, why he was so nervous to pull a little prank. But I knew he was still up for some sort of mischief despite his past. What had he said yesterday? Something about being addicted to the mystery. He wouldn't be trying to use his skills for good as a spy if he wasn't.

I finished tying my shoes and made myself busy with my backpack, making sure everything we might need was in there. Just like Emily and her Backpack of Everything, you never knew what you would need. Emily Steinfeld might even make a great agent. Why wouldn't they recruit her? Or Amelia? I made a mental note to propose the idea to Ms. Blanchard. Did they take recommendations?

Ethan was on the lake for his canoe lesson. Bentley finished tying his boots and left the cabin, Oliss right behind him. Handel dropped the comic and peaked out the window.

"They're gone," he said.

"Perfect. Our diversion is in place?" I slung my bag over my shoulder as Handel nodded.

Handel skimmed over the file one last time before we stepped out the door and headed across the field. "Ethan knows what to do?" he asked.

I nodded. The night before, we got Ethan to join our mission. His class wasn't scheduled to perform their mission drills until next week. He would cause the perfect diversion for us, but he didn't share exactly what that would be.

To complete our retrieval mission, we had to find that flash drive and bring it to Agent P.R. before our time was up. We had two days. It shouldn't take us more than a few hours.

"Where are you two heading?" Oliss asked.

I spun around. Oliss was only a few feet away from me. I thought he left. He sauntered over to us, leaving his perch beside the cabin wall.

"Just going to grab a banana from the cafeteria," I said. He didn't look convinced. "Then we were going to go study history."

"I'll join you," he said. "Bentley is running a couple laps before we start our combat training."

"No problem." I smiled and we turned towards the cafeteria. Something was wrong. Oliss hated hanging out with us. I glanced at Handel, and the slightest nod told me I was right. He was trying to interfere with our mission. We needed to get rid of him. Think, Tony, think!

I grabbed a banana off the counter when we got to the cafeteria. Catching Handel's attention, I nodded towards Oliss, trying to convey my message without words. Whether or not he understood, he acted. Handel turned to Oliss and asked questions about his combat techniques. Oliss could never miss a chance to sound smart or drill someone about the need for fighting. When he was distracted, I slipped off to the bathroom, dropping the banana in a trash can on the way. If I headed for the door, it would have been too obvious.

I passed the urinals and stopped by the only window in the room.

The window was about two inches higher than my arms could reach, and I was tall. I looked around for something to stand on, but there wasn't anything. Standing on my toes, I was able to slide the glass open with my fingertips. I reached up to pop out the screen, straining. My toes burned as I forced myself to reach higher. "There we go," I whispered when the screen gave way and fell to the ground outside. I tossed my backpack through. I measured how much energy I would need to make the jump, finally glad all the PT would pay off. Maybe there was a reason for all the pull ups.

After taking a few quick breaths, pumping myself up, I jumped. My fingers grasped the windowsill. I pulled myself up. Squeezing through the opening, I tumbled onto the grass. "Didn't think about the landing," I huffed, pulling myself to my feet and dusting off my pants. Handel was on his own, and so was I.

Next stop? The infirmary.

"Can I help you, Mr. Anderson?" Dr. Powell asked when I rushed inside. I took in the small waiting room and the doctor behind the desk.

I didn't have to fake the heavy breaths as I grasped my knees. "It's Ethan. He's at the lake. There was a canoeing accident."

"That doesn't sound good." Dr. Powell jumped from his chair and ran out the door.

The moment the front door shut, I slipped behind his desk and searched. In the drawers, between the papers, under the desk. There wasn't a single flash drive. It had to be somewhere in the back. I tried the only door in the waiting room, but it was locked. I rifled through the desk again, but there was no key. My backpack.

I slipped off the straps and went through everything that I packed. We had been allowed to take three gadgets with us from class. There was a laser pen, a mini taser, and a decoding device. Other than that, was my pencil case, two flash drives I was ready to use as decoys, and a notebook. What was I supposed to do?

"Come on," I whined, making a fist. I should have chosen better equipment.

The front door slipped open. I froze, my heart rate jumping. Handel shut the door behind him, locking it.

"How did you get rid of Oliss?" I asked, momentarily forgetting about my problem. It probably would have helped to know how to get into the back room beforehand.

"He kept asking where you were, and when he went to the bathroom to look for you, I slipped away. For being such a skilled fighter, he doesn't know how to distract someone. Did you find it?"

"It's not here and I can't get into the back room. If it were a computer password locking me out, I would have been in already. If only there was a gadget for this type of thing." I frowned, frustrated for not thinking this through. Handel tried the door for himself, then went through the desk like I had. I shook my head as he searched. "There isn't a key. Dr. Powell probably had it on his person."

"I don't need a key." Handel rifled through the drawers a couple more moments before pulling out two paper clips. "I got this." He crouched by the door handle.

Why didn't I think about picking the lock? I've never tried something like that before. Handel bent the paper clips and worked them inside the lock until it clicked.

"You have to teach me how to do that," I said. Handel smiled, and we slipped inside.

Chapter 20

Anything Can be a Gadget

There was a small hallway with four doors. I peeked through the first one, but it was just a bathroom. Across the hallway was a small supply closet. The third door, beside the closet, opened into the hospital room. We slipped inside and searched the place.

"There isn't anything here," Handel said. He rifled through the last cabinet above the counter. I dug through the last two drawers before I gave up.

"You're right." The room was empty. There was all the medical equipment you could need in the drawers and the supply closet, but not a flash drive. "There's one more door we can try."

I followed Handel down the hallway to the last door. **Dr. Powell** was written on the plaque.

"It's open," Handel whispered, turning the knob. It was Dr. Powell's office. It was the messiest office I had ever seen.

A couch occupied the wall beside the door, pillows and blankets thrown across it. The coffee table had two mugs on it and a mess of papers and magazines.

The desk sat in the middle of the room, cluttered bookshelves standing behind it. His desk had piles of files, books scattered across it and two mugs filled with pens and pencils. Two chairs faced his desk, and they were the only pieces of furniture not covered in something.

"You would think doctors would be more organized," I said. Handel nodded, his mouth slightly open in shock at the state of the place. "Come on. Let's start searching."

I headed for the desk while Handel scoured through the shelves. The mugs didn't hold anything useful. I sorted through the papers as best I could without knocking anything over. It was like an organized mess. Everything had a place; you just didn't know where it was.

Thud.

Handel jerked back to look at me. "Sorry," I whispered.

A book had slid off the edge of the desk before I could catch it. Handel put the books in his hands back on the shelf and moved to the filing cabinet below him.

I opened the first drawer to the same organized mess that was on the desk. Paperclips, safety pins, medicine bottles, and more slid around as I opened the second drawer. There were files in it, but nothing more. The last drawer slid open slowly. It was heavy.

"Handel." I waved him over and we knelt by the opened drawer. There was a safe taking up the drawer space with a four-digit lock combination.

I slipped my backpack off and pulled out the decoder. I worked fast, attaching the device and watching it spin through all possible number combinations until the lock clicked open. "Being a spy is going to be awesome," I said, shoving the device back in my bag.

"Let's finish the mission before we celebrate, okay?" Handel opened the safe.

Inside were a couple files, two prescription bottles, and a small case. I pulled out the case and zipped it open.

"Can we celebrate now?" I asked, pulling out a flash drive. Handel glared at me, but I kept on smiling. We had found it.

I tucked the flash drive in my backpack, placing a decoy inside the safe. Opening the door to the hallway, my feet stopped in their tracks.

"Where do you think you're going?"

I froze, one foot in the doorway and one in the hall. Agent Mills stood in the middle of the hallway with her arms crossed.

The moment stretched, stilled. Then Agent Mills moved. She charged us. I darted back inside the office, shutting the door behind me.

"What do we do?" I asked, leaning against the door. Agent Mills only tried to open it once. It was terrifying not knowing what she was doing out there.

"There's no other way out of here," Handel said. "We're going to have to overpower her."

"Have you seen her fight?" I asked. "She kicked me in the gut on day one. She hates me!" Handel shrugged. I looked around the room for something. Anything. I took a short breath, nodding to myself. "I have an idea."

On three, I mouthed. Handel nodded from his crouched position by the coffee table. *One*...Handel clutched the book he grabbed from the shelf. *Two*...I nodded, running through the plan in my head. *Three*.

I unlocked the door, froze to see if Agent Mills would barrel through it. I turned the knob and opened it. With barely enough time to get out of the way, the door burst open. The moment Mills barged through, Handel threw the book at her. She sidestepped, the book hitting the door behind her. Agent Mills smiled at Handel. Handel's face turned pale, just for a moment before he grabbed another book. I slipped through the door and into the hallway, leaving Handel with Agent Mills.

Crashing erupted from Dr. Powell's office. I ducked into the hospital room and closed the door behind me. A shout drifted down the hallway as I made sure the door was locked. Throwing open the supply closet, I grabbed the IV bags and separated the tubes from the bags. More shouting came from the end of the hall as I finished tying loops in the ends of them.

"Anderson!" Agent Mills stormed down the hallway. Her voice was right outside the door. "You know I blocked the only exit." She tried the handle, but it wouldn't open for her. I scrambled to put the last thing I needed in place, stealing a look at the doorknob as it jiggled. Her footsteps drifted a little, and I opened the door.

"In here!" I shouted.

She ran from the front office and into the room. I had placed the rolling stool in front of the door and an IV bag on the floor, right where she would step. Agent Mills barreled into the room, tripped on the bag of fluid and fell onto the stool. It took her flying across the room. I slammed the door shut behind her before she could stand up.

The hospital had an odd setup, but it worked to my advantage. The door to the hospital room I was in stood beside the door to a mini supply closet. The door handles were only a foot apart, the supply closet door mirroring the hospital room door instead of both opening in the same direction.

Using the IV tube I had removed earlier, I slipped one loop over each door handle and tightened them with a knot between the doors. I tugged on it, nodding at the tightness in the tube.

When Agent Mills tried to open the door, the tension from the IV tube looped around the other door would keep her from opening it. The drip tube on the end of the piping swung below the closet door handle. She was locked in.

The hospital room's handle jiggled. I jumped. It opened a few inches, but not enough to get through. I smiled, the IV tube working to keep it shut.

"Anderson!" Agent Mills shouted from inside.

My heartbeat quickened at the sound of her anger. I jumped with excitement. The door wouldn't open, not easily with the tension of the two doors fighting against each other. Agent Mills was stuck inside.

Back in the lobby, I found Handel sitting on the couch in Dr. Powell's office.

"Are you okay?" I asked.

"All good." He held his arms, but he was smiling. "Dr. Powell won't be happy when he sees his office though."

I smiled. "Let's finish this."

Agent Mills had blocked the front door with the couch. Her shouts of anger fueled me as we pushed it aside. I heard the doorknobs rattling as we left the infirmary.

Back in the Logistical Tactics classroom, Agent P.R. sat at a desk in the front of the room with a paper in his hand.

"Mission accomplished, sir," I said, placing the flash drive on the desk in front of him.

"Tony and Handel…" his voice drifted off as his eyes darted across his page. "Your retrieval mission was to locate and retrieve a flash drive in Dr. Powell's possession." He looked at the flash drive and smiled. "Well done boys."

"We did it?" Handel asked.

"Yes, you did. You finished your first mission. Congrats."

"Thanks," I said, unable to wipe the smile off my face.

Agent P.R. pocketed the flash drive and checked off a box on his paper. "Enjoy the rest of your weekend. You two were the first to finish your assignment."

Handel nodded. I returned the gadgets we borrowed for the mission and opened the door to leave.

Agent Mills stood right in front of us.

"Smart," she said, crossing her arms. "Way to use the things around you, guys."

I nodded, and she stepped inside the classroom before I let the door close.

Chapter 21

Agent Z

"You seriously jumped through the bathroom window?" Oliss asked when we met up in the dining hall for dinner.

"What did you want me to do? You have never tried to talk to me so much since I met you." I shoved a couple French fries into my mouth.

Oliss huffed. "I guess it was a pretty good escape."

I snickered as he looked down at his plate. He wasn't exactly good at distractions either. We all had our weaknesses. Maybe Mr. Big Shot on campus needed some improvement in his spy skills too.

The conversation changed when Handel and Ethan started debating the abilities of two comic book characters and which would win in battle against Agent Mills. I laughed and glanced around the room; my attention being pulled towards the instructors' table.

Agent Mills' phone rang. She furrowed her brow at it, picked it up, then left the cafeteria.

On instinct, I stood to follow her. "Where are you going?" Ethan asked.

"I'll be right back."

"That's not an answer!" Ethan yelled after me.

Agent Mills disappeared around the cabin next door, the phone to her ear. I ducked behind the building, just within earshot.

"You're right, Z. We need him." Agent Mills said. She sighed and nodded. "I know. I just don't want anyone else to get hurt. These kids are not ready for what's coming."

Who was Z? I leaned in closer, wishing I could hear who was on the other side of that phone.

"You should have seen how he locked me in there. It was genius." She was talking about me, she had to be. "Alright. I'll recruit him, but I will not make him join us unless he wants to. This isn't his fight." She paused. "Bye, Agent Z." Agent Mills hung up the phone and shoved it in her pocket.

I ducked behind the building.

"Anderson!" I froze. "I know you're there, Anderson. Get out here!"

I shut my eyes. She was good. I sighed as I stepped into her line of sight.

"Hi."

"So, we've resorted to spying on our instructors now, have we?" She tugged down on her fingerless gloves and crossed her arms.

"Listen," I started.

"I'm all ears."

"Something is going on here, and I need to know what it is." I pushed my worry away. She wasn't my father, she would listen. She didn't rat me out for the smoke bomb. She was a good sport when I locked her in the hospital room. "You're planning something. I can tell. I don't know if it's good or bad, but I can't help but ask."

"What exactly do you think I'm doing?"

"Umm." An awkward silence passed between us.

Agent Mills sighed. "It's alright, Tony," she said. "You're right, I'm hiding something. It's time you're filled in."

"Who is Agent Z?" I asked, stepping closer.

"If I told you the true identity of an agent, I would be breaking a huge law in the T.S.O." Agent Mills smirked. I was ready to back off when she said, "All rules aside, I was given permission to tell you." She smiled. "Agent Z is also known as Amelia Zegro."

"Zegro?" She had to be talking about someone else, right? Amelia? Amelia from Glayfield? It was impossible. "Prove it." I crossed my arms.

"Fine." With that, Agent Mills walked away.

"Where are you going?" I shouted.

Agent Mills pulled a flash drive out of her pocket and waved it in the air. "Don't you want answers?"

I followed Agent Mills inside a cabin.

"This is the flash drive you were assigned to retrieve," Agent Mills said, plugging it into a computer. We sat inside a classroom behind the teacher's desk. "Part of your test was to see if you would be too curious and look at its contents without permission."

"Is that really something you think I would do?"

Agent Mills smirked. "You made your own smoke bomb. You pepper me with questions during training yet still seem to hold back. There is something about you Tony. Yes, I thought you were capable of it." She turned back to the computer. "I know I sure am."

I shrugged. It had been tempting, but in that moment, finishing the assignment had seemed more important. As I thought back on it, it had barely crossed my mind.

"You're not like this at home, are you?"

There was a pause. "No," I said, refusing to look at her. "My father acts like I do nothing right. I can't get a word in without making him angry. At home I'm no one of importance."

"Well, here, you ask all the questions you can think of. Don't stop doing that, okay?" Alexis turned and looked at me. "You just have to learn when to ask the right ones."

The smile I gave her was forced. Why did I admit that to her?

The file from the flash drive opened, saving me from embarrassment. I looked at the content she pulled up on the computer. A video file popped up. As Agent Mills played the video, my brain full of questions was ready to explode.

"What is this?" I asked, anger rising in my throat.

"This is a video your friends Amelia Zegro and Emily Steinfeld retrieved from Savannah Bakers. This was the proof we needed to help put Jason Bakers, also known as Dr. Doom, behind bars. He was responsible for the accident that led to Amelia's memory loss. Among other crimes."

"You're joking, right?" I asked, leaning closer to the computer.

The video began. It was Savannah Bakers, a classmate from school. She was with a man that looked old enough to be her father.

"Savannah, you can't back out now!" The man shouted. He said something about a weapon. "None of this would have happened if it wasn't for you."

I kept watching as Savannah seemed to deflate. The man shouted once more. "She knew too much! It had to be done. Just be glad she isn't dead."

Agent Mills stopped the video. She turned to look at me, but I couldn't look away from the screen. This girl played a part in hurting Amelia. How could I not have known? I spent every day with them at school. How could I not tell Amelia was a secret agent? Why didn't I know my friend was in danger?

"Tony, Amelia gave me permission to tell you her identity, to show you this."

I stood up and paced across the room.

Amelia's accident was connected to the T.S.O.?

Agent Mills kept talking. I listened, everything slowly starting to make sense. She told me about Amelia's accident, Emily and Amelia being part of the T.S.O. and meeting Agent Mills when they were in Training Camp. She said Amelia was responsible for arresting Dr. Doom. She talked about a Bayshire Stone and someone named Mr. Bard. Her story sounded weirder and weirder.

She couldn't be lying. The video on the flash drive, this Dr. Doom talking to Savannah about someone who was obviously Amelia, was proof of that.

"Why are you telling me all of this?" I asked, rubbing my temples.

"Because we need you. The T.S.O. is in trouble, Tony."

"How? Why me?" I sat back down in my seat, feeling overwhelmed.

Agent Mills was quiet for a moment. She huffed, scrunched her face, then she pulled down on her gloves. She did that an awful lot. "There are people inside the T.S.O. that want to ruin us, what we stand for. We don't know who we can trust." She drifted for a moment.

"Agent Mills."

"Right." Agent Mills stood up and started pacing, talking with her hands. "We have moles in the organization, Tony. We don't know how deep it runs or who they're working for. Emily and Amelia are working with me and my crew to figure out what these people are planning. We're close, but not knowing who we can trust is keeping us from digging much further. Ms. Blanchard is working around the clock to stop these people before they act, but I think we're running out of time. My sources tell me whatever these traitors are planning is going to happen soon."

"And what does all of this have to do with me?"

"I've been watching you these past few weeks, Anderson. You're smart, creative. You think outside the box and that's what we need right now." Agent Mills smirked at me. I pushed down the heat rising to my cheeks. "We might be strong already, but we need someone with a different perspective. Someone who isn't so close to this already. You have no past with the T.S.O. That alone makes you trustworthy, not to mention all your other skills. I mean, you built a freaking smoke grenade out of garden supplies and trash. You locked me in a hospital with an IV tube. Who does that?"

"You taught us to use our surroundings. That's what I did."

"Exactly!" she said, pointing a finger at me. "Amelia told me about some of the pranks you've pulled before. We could use your skills, Anderson. What do you say?"

I wrapped my mind around the idea of traitors in an organization I had only known about for a couple months. How long had my friends been keeping a secret like this from me? I couldn't blame them, but it still hurt. The thought of someone deliberately wanting to hurt Amelia made me want to punch something.

"You say I can help," I said, my voice as flat as sandpaper. "But you don't know me. I'm the guy that everyone ignores. I'm not useful. At home, I'm only ever in the way. You don't want me covering your back in a fight. I'll just mess things up."

Agent Mills sighed, hands on her hips. "How about this? I'll give you some private lessons. We can start tomorrow. We'll work on building your combat skills as long as you promise not to make the next bomb purple." She paused, looking at me pointedly. "You're not useless."

I couldn't smile at her joke. The thought of training one-on-one with Agent Mills didn't sit well. She could kill me before I moved if she wanted to. I didn't see how my ability to pull pranks would be helpful.

Memories of my mother ran through my mind. She made sure I had the skills I did, but they were in chemistry not combat. Still, I never let myself forget.

Maybe.

Just maybe, if I survived training with Agent Mills, I would be able to do something about whatever war Agent Mills was bent on fighting. I could do something my parents might be proud of.

You're not useless.

I repeated her words in my head, holding onto them. I had to help. If I didn't, something worse could happen to my friends.

"Deal?" Agent Mills asked.

I looked at her, and for the second time this year, I decided to be a part of something bigger than myself.

"Deal."

Chapter 22

Agent Mills' Rock Music

The next morning, I arrived at the gym at exactly five-thirty. As soon as I stepped onto the mat, Agent Mills entered from the girl's locker room. I really didn't understand why she would train in a leather jacket, but I wasn't going to ask. I didn't need to get kicked in the ribs again.

"Ready to get started?" she asked.

"I guess." I shrugged my shoulders.

"There is no 'I guess.'" Agent Mills said. She walked to the edge of the mat. "You like music?" I was going to say "I guess" but decided against it. Agent Mills picked up her phone from the side of the mat. "You can't fight without the proper music."

"Whatever you say."

Agent Mills laughed an unsettling laugh. She set down her phone near a speaker. Music filled the space. The song was fast paced and intense. I had no idea what song it was.

"Much better." Agent Mills tugged on her fingerless gloves and gave me a smile. "Now, today we'll work on combat."

"Fighting isn't my strong suit," I said, positioning my feet on the mat.

"No, it's not."

Agent Mills threw her fist towards me. Before I realized what I was doing, I used my arm to deflect her punch, stepping out of her hitting range. "But you will learn." She threw another punch, this time stepping into it. I deflected her punch again, twisting on the mat. I turned to look at her just in time to see her foot sweep across the mat. I jumped back, but she spun around and grabbed my shirt collar.

Breathing was hard already. Her brown eyes stared into mine, but I was too shocked to try and step back. Thankfully, she let go of my shirt and moved away.

"We've got some work to do."

And that's exactly what we did. She didn't attack me again. Agent Mills led me through stretches and exercises, then guided me through an explanation of the main pressure points on the body. After that she explained various attack and defense maneuvers. She was very calm, very patient. I would've thought it was a completely different person if it wasn't for her frequent sarcastic comments and remarks. She was patient in class but couldn't really pay this much attention to one person in a group setting.

After an hour, it was time to stop. I was sweating like crazy, but it felt good. I was smiling. With my chest pounding, I was ready to head back to the cabin to change but stopped myself before I lost my chance.

"Can I ask you something?"

Agent Mills nodded. "Shoot."

"You fell off the rock wall, right?"

"Duh." She gave me a quizzical look.

"I was just wondering. What happened?"

"Well," Agent Mills sat down on the mat. She turned off the music and took a swig from her water bottle. I came and sat a few feet in front of her. "I fell. There isn't much more to it. I got really hurt. Had to basically sit out of all physical classes for the rest of camp. I had to get surgery on my leg."

I couldn't help but glance down at her leg, but the scar was covered by her pants.

"Does it hurt?" I asked.

Agent Mills sighed, looking at me pointedly. "Let me tell you something. When you get hurt, you can't give up. No matter what you do, your scars are still going to be there. All you can do is make yourself stronger from it. You learn to accept what happened and use it. If you don't, others might use your weakness to their advantage."

"What do you mean?"

Agent Mills sighed and flicked her hair back. "My last case, well, it wasn't technically my case I guess, but that's a different story. Anyway, I was ambushed and someone who knew about my accident used it against me. If it wasn't for someone else's help, I wouldn't have finished my mission."

"That's pretty good advice, actually. Thanks." I wanted to know more, but I didn't want to pry. Agent Mills had already opened up to me, and apparently my curiosity was something she paid attention to. What was I supposed to say? I had no deep secrets to divulge or dark pasts that haunted me at night. I was an open book. Wasn't I?

"No problem," she said. "You should probably go for breakfast though."

"One more question." I thought for a moment about how to approach the subject. I wanted to know who she was talking to on the phone other than Agent Z. Who was on her team? I had agreed to help, now I needed to know what I was up against. But if I brought it up, she would know I was listening in on her first phone call. I needed her to trust me. "You know what, never mind."

"You sure?" She raised her eyebrows at me.

"I'm sure."

"See you in class then." Agent Mills stood and headed for the locker room.

I stood up and left the gym. Part of me didn't know if I could actually trust Agent Mills. It was a horrible feeling. She knew my friends, and I trusted them, even if they were secret agents and never told me. If Agent Mills was evil, she wouldn't be training me. I had to figure out what was going on.

Chapter 23

Unlocking T.S.O.

In Gadgetry I was a little confused when I sat down. On my desk was a hand-held lock and a credit card. What was I supposed to do? Go shopping?

I was sore from training this morning, but I didn't care. The fact that Agent Mills was privately training me still boggled my mind. I wanted to call Amelia, talk to her and get all my answers, but communication with the outside world was prohibited for agents-in-training.

"Alright everyone," Agent P.R. started. "Today you will learn how to use the little gadget on each of your desks." I looked at the lock, then the card. Which one was the gadget?

"The key card is a gadget every agent is given when they graduate from camp. It's a rather ingenious device."

I picked up the credit card and turned it over in my hand. A key card?

"Does anyone have any ideas as to what this device is?" Agent P.R. asked.

I slid my finger across the numbers on the card, then flipped it over again. It wasn't a credit card. I knew that much, considering it was sitting on my desk. Rubbing my fingers over the numbers again, one of them moved under my touch. I picked up the lock and examined it. It needed a key, and I was holding it in my hand.

I pushed down on the number on the card. A green light shot out from the side of the card, and I moved it in front of the lock.

Agent P.R. walked over to my desk.

It was a scanner. I moved the green light to scan the keyhole on the lock, then the front half of the credit card folded in on itself. It turned into a key. Agent P.R. smiled at me as I jammed the key into the lock and turned it. Was that the coolest thing ever, or what? That would have been useful when I was breaking into the infirmary.

"Very good, Tony," my teacher said. He walked back to the front of the class and explained what I just did. "Now, here is the important thing to remember," he said. "A key card is very useful, but it does have its disadvantages. Once used, it takes the card about an hour to recharge before you can use it again."

I left class with a skip in my step. So far today had been going pretty well. First, I trained with Agent Mills, then I aced Gadgetry class.

The rest of the day whizzed by. When my free period arrived, I planned to go swimming. On my way towards the dock, I spotted Oliss and Bentley sparring on a mat by the volleyball court. Maybe I could use their help. I changed course and headed towards them.

The next thing I knew I was dodging punches from Oliss. My training with Agent Mills from that morning ran through my mind, and I played defense as best I could. Half an hour later I was coated in sweat and smiling. I had even managed to land a punch.

"Good enough," Oliss said. "For your first fight, anyways."

Was that a compliment? I wasn't sure. I stretched out my leg where Oliss had kicked me.

"I'm going to grab some water. Be right back." Oliss left and I turned towards Bentley. He shook his head and sighed.

"What?" I asked. I watched Oliss cross the clearing and disappear between the trees.

"He's too hard on himself," Bentley said. His voice was deep. It was the first time I had heard him speak.

"I can tell."

"His brother is an agent," Bentley said. "He thinks he has to be just as good as him, just as strong." I didn't respond. Bentley waved his finger at me to spar again.

Chapter 24

Meetings, Convicts, and Traitors, Oh My!

I wandered around camp before heading to my next class. I was replaying the last time I saw Amelia, wondering how she was connected to all this, when voices pushed the memory out of my head.

I stopped walking, my feet glued to the grass. I had wandered closer to the woods where we weren't allowed to go alone. There were voices coming from a cabin that was off the path, hidden in a cluster of trees. Wooden panels and windows peaked out of the foliage, begging me to step closer so I could understand the noise.

"No, Tony," I said.

There had to be a way to figure out what was going on without getting into trouble. But getting into trouble was what I was good at.

I crept along the side of the cabin. The windows were open, and voices drifted out into the air.

It was the Director.

Ms. Blanchard's voice was full of lead, demanding and grounded. Even so, it was too soft for me to make out what she was saying.

I had to get a closer look. What was the director talking about? Who was she talking to? I crept further around the cabin, closer to an open window as her voice got louder.

Bam!

I walked right into Agent Mills. What was she doing here?

"Agent Mills?"

"Shh!"

She grabbed my arm and pulled me further along the side of the building. She peeked her head through a window above us. Was I supposed to do the same? I risked a look, wanting to know what was so important it made Agent Mills spy on the director, not that I wasn't already doing that on my own.

The walls were wood. Inside the room was a long table. At the end of the room, Ms. Blanchard paced back and forth. A giant TV screen hung on the wall. The screen showed a man who had to be much older than Ms. Blanchard, frowning at her through the TV.

"Dr. Doom is a huge risk," Ms. Blanchard said. "This is unacceptable."

Agent Mills grabbed my arm and pulled me down as Ms. Blanchard turned in our direction. Dr. Doom was the guy Agent Mills said hurt Amelia Zegro. I felt the urge to punch the guy. I thought about Agent Mills and her secret phone calls. This is what she's been doing! Agent Mills has been spying on the director the whole time.

"Doom is the least of our worries," the man on the screen said. I held my breath and strained my neck to hear. "You have directors threatening to go public just to save their own skin. I can't hold back the press for much longer."

"Sir." Ms. Blanchard stopped pacing and faced the man. "The T.S.O. is secret for a reason. You have let us work in private for years without a single problem. I can't control the actions of other directors, but I can control the agents that work under me."

The man on the screen sighed. "Ms. Blanchard, you're dealing with moles in your own organization. This has to take priority over escaped convicts and missing artifacts."

"What do you want me to do? Some of my best agents are at risk here. Doom is bound to go after Agent Z. And the measures that Agent Mills and Agent Watson took just to retrieve the Bayshire can't be overlooked. That stone is dangerous. Everything is connected to Doom. That much I know for certain."

Agent Mills balled her fists and shook her head. The muscles in her face tightened.

"Look, I can't tell you how to run your agency," the man said. "I have funded you since you first came to me. I'm just trying to help."

Agent Mills grabbed my arm and pulled me away from the building. She started running, dragging me along with her. Was this what she wanted my help with? Whatever the director was angry about?

"What the heck is going on?" I shouted, knowing I was far enough from the cabin to say something. "Why is she talking about your case?"

Agent Mills didn't answer. She continued pulling me away from the cabins, away from the lake. Then I realized what she was doing. Agent Mills was leading me towards the woods.

Chapter 25

If It's Easy, It's a Trap

Once we were covered by a line of trees, Agent Mills let go of me.

"Please explain what I just heard," I said.

Agent Mills was walking in circles, her hands on her head, then on her hips. Has she always been this wound up?

"This isn't good. I was really hoping I was wrong."

"What isn't good?" I needed answers. "Are my friends in danger?" Agent Mills didn't answer any of my questions. "Doom—that's the guy you were telling me about, right?"

Finally, Agent Mills stopped pacing. She stared at me, trying to figure out where to start. Agent Z was Amelia. The director said she could be in danger. And something about the T.S.O. going public.

"Dr. Doom is the man who put Amelia in the hospital, who took her memory," I clarified. I had to make sure my facts were right, at least the ones that I already had.

"I helped capture him a while ago," Agent Mills started. "You see, Amelia and Emily were trying to keep him from breaking his brother out of jail. When we caught him though, we realized he was trying to break out his old partner, not his brother. Dr. Doom had another accomplice hidden inside the T.S.O. He was the first mole we discovered. Ms. Blanchard thinks everything is connected. But what are they planning?" She said the last part under her breath.

"Moles. Okay, bad," I clarified. "Dr. Doom is evil, but what does that have to do with the director? And remind me again what a Bayshire is."

"The Bayshire is a stone capable of generating extremely dangerous levels of electricity. My last case was to retrieve it from a man named Randall Bard. Long story short, I ended up coming all the way to California to get it. When I got here, I realized what had happened to Agent Z, and she and Stienfeld ended up helping me retrieve the stone. Dr. Doom wanted it. Savannah told us about it, and we got it before he could. He was put in jail, and I finished my mission. Ms. Blanchard doesn't know about Mr. Bard. I should have told her about his threat." Agent Mills paused. "Hold on. I need to think."

Agent Mills started pacing again, and I struggled to put the puzzle together. Mr. Bard was the guy who owned the stone. And Dr. Doom had wanted it. An idea started to form in my head, and I didn't like it.

"What if…" I trailed off and Agent Mills kept pacing. "Ms. Blanchard thinks everything is somehow connected, right? What if Doom and Mr. Bard are working together?" I asked.

Agent Mills froze. She tilted her head. "There's a scary thought." She squinted and somehow looked even more worried. "You might actually be on to something."

"Really?" Even though a dreadful taste filled my mouth, I smiled.

"It was too easy."

"What was too easy?" I asked.

"It was too easy! Getting the stone," Agent Mills said. Her eyes widened. When a teenager who can take you down in less than thirty seconds turns on you with a wild look in her eyes, you don't exactly feel comfortable.

"In Glayfield," she explained as she began pacing again. "There was no security at the museum. We just grabbed the stone and left. It was too easy. Tony, I think you're right."

"Okay."

I frowned, my eyes following her as she paced in front of me. Agent Mills had told me about her last case, but she left out any details about security. Whatever she was talking about, she was onto something. I nodded, encouraging her to keep going.

"That's why Mr. Bard was so angry on the train. He was working with Doom. He had no security detail in California like he did the other places because he made it easy for Doom to get the stone. The entire tour was just a cover! He wasn't expecting me to go after it."

"But what about Ms. Blanchard worrying about Doom, about Amelia being in danger? And who is Agent Watson?" I gestured as I talked, matching Agent Mills' level of excitement.

"First off, Watson is a total weasel. But if Doom escaped from prison, then she's right. Amelia is in danger. This guy holds serious grudges. Based on what Mr. Bard said on the train, the T.S.O. is in a lot more danger than just going public."

"What did Mr. Bard say on the train?"

"He told me I would pay for what I've done." The energy seemed to fade from her eyes. "He knows about the T.S.O. He said he has friends who would want to know about us." Agent Mills looked past me into the trees, lost in her memory.

"This isn't good," I said. "He must know who the moles are. He has a plan of some sort."

"Tony, listen." Agent Mills shook her head, focusing on me again.

"I'm listening."

"Amelia and Emily said the director was acting strange. But she was just worried. She was worried about Agent Z, and she was worried about me not getting the stone in time. She can only do so much without raising eyebrows. Other directors would question her motives. It would cause unrest in the Board, leaving the T.S.O. weak. Doom and Mr. Bard have to be planning something."

"But the director said something about moles, about going public. That seems like two separate problems."

Agent Mills froze. Her eyebrows rose in an aha! moment. "No, they aren't. I hate that I'm right."

Me too, I thought.

"Who's the mole then?"

Agent Mills looked at me, dead serious.

"Miles."

Chapter 26

Directors

During our next training session, I forced myself to work harder. It didn't matter how much it hurt. I needed to be able to help. Agent Mills didn't explain who Miles was, but that was fine. I had enough floating around in my head to worry about.

As soon as we took a break, I asked Agent Mills a question that had been nagging at me for a while.

"A couple days ago I might have overheard you talking on the phone with someone," I said.

Agent Mills put down her water bottle and stared at me. Uh-oh. "You were spying on me?" She tilted her head. "Of course you were spying on me."

"I want to know what was going on."

Alexis nodded. "I was talking to Tanner, my partner. Ever since I got back from my last case, Agent Watson, Tanner, and myself have been trying to figure out what the director was up to. Watson and I figured the case we were on wasn't planned properly. And that was Mr. Martial's fault."

"Who's Mr. Martial?"

"My boss. The director of the Ohio base." Last night's conversation made me uneasy. The guy in the video said other directors wanted to go public. It sounded like Ms. Blanchard was losing control.

"Everything I learned about having traitors in the organization only added to the confusion." Agent Mills tugged on her gloves. "We thought the director was the traitor. Tanner has been keeping an eye on things back at Ohio, and I have been trying to figure out Ms. Blanchard's motives since camp started."

Agent Mills said I was important before. But I didn't get it. I wasn't a good fighter. I was too self-conscious. Even my dad didn't want me around.

"Why bring me into this?" I asked.

"I figured you would be willing to help, especially if you knew your friends were involved. And when the time comes, I need as many allies as I can get. Miles tried to get me on his side without giving anything away. I don't understand why yet, but he wants the T.S.O. to be public knowledge. And Mr. Martial might be in on it too. You have good skills, skills we all might need."

"But I'm obviously not the best at combat. We've been training for days. What skills do I have that you and your friends don't?" I hated what I said, but it was true. I wasn't a good fighter, and it was obvious.

"No, but you think outside the box. I already told you that. You have good instincts," Agent Mills said.

"Thanks?"

"Don't mention it. Come on, let's get back to work."

Chapter 27

Who Runs the Show? Not Us.

I spent the next couple days absorbed in my training, learning from Agent Mills. She told me about her last case, every detail. It really was a long story. Agent Mills traveled to California to get the Bayshire Stone against orders to leave it alone. She explained to me everything she learned about the director with Amelia and Emily and about her friends Agent Watson and Tanner, or Agent B. She never referred to Agent Watson by his first name.

I trained even harder with her. I spent my free time training, sometimes with Oliss. The more time I spent with him, the more I understood him. He wasn't mean, just hard on himself. Oliss and Bentley were both from Ohio and had met last year at camp. They were like brothers.

During gadgetry class I memorized every little detail. I did the same in all my classes. Any piece of information I could use was helpful. Agent Mills didn't know what was going to happen or what we'd need to prepare for. We never caught Ms. Blanchard in any secret meetings again. Come to think of it, we didn't really see her at all. It was like she disappeared into the woods.

A routine emerged. Train in the morning, I go to class, train with Agent Mills, train in my free time, brainstorm what was going to happen. A week had gone by since we stumbled upon Ms. Blanchard's private meeting. We weren't getting anywhere, until today when breakfast was served.

It was hot out today. There was still a month left at camp. A month to figure out what was going on before I got sent back into the real world. I was replaying my combat session from earlier that morning in my mind, how Agent Mills took me down with a leg sweep I hadn't anticipated. There had to have been a better way to get out of that.

"Attention please!"

The thought was cut short when the buzzing from a microphone crackled through the cafeteria. Agent Powell stood in front of the instructors' table, microphone in hand. The room went silent.

"Attention agents," Agent Powell said. I shifted in my seat. No one had called me an agent before. It felt oddly satisfying. "Today we will begin training on the rock wall. After lunch, all classes will be canceled for full-camp-instruction. With preparations for the obstacle course competition in a week and outdoor survival for year-two campers, it's time to bring everyone's training to the next level."

He cleared his throat and continued. "The rock wall can be a very dangerous form of training so we will start slowly. I will be on site at all times for medical emergencies. Agent Mills and Agent Q will lead the drill."

My Defense Tactics instructor and Physical Training instructor were teaming up. That was going to be a wonderful combination. This was not going to be easy. Then

I made the mistake of looking at Agent Mills. She was staring right at me. She mouthed something, but she was too far away for me to make anything out. There was something else she had to tell me.

"Finally," Oliss said.

"Have you done it before?" Handel asked. "I saw the wall. It doesn't look easy."

"It's not." Oliss shook his head. "Last year I never made it to the top without falling. But Agent Mills as our teacher? That will be interesting." By now we had all learned about her accident. The fact that I caught her on the wall before by herself, unharnessed, was surprising enough. But guiding agents-in-training on the wall? Agent Mills acted like she didn't have a single limit. Like superman, only without kryptonite. Everyone had a weakness. I had no idea what hers was.

After History, I headed straight for the rock wall. My stomach crawled into my throat, and I was afraid I wouldn't be able to keep anything down. I had a feeling I wasn't the only one.

"Mr. Curious." Agent Mills was already at the wall. I hated the nickname, but she wasn't wrong. "Can't eat either?" she asked. I shook my head. "Give me a moment." Agent Mills finished tying a rope attached to the wall to a pad on the ground. When she finished, she stepped off the safety mat and headed to a pile of harnesses laid out on the ground. "I need to talk to you," she said.

"I figured. Agent Mills, did you find out anything else about Dr. Doom or Ms. Blanchard?"

"Hand me that rope," she replied, "And it's Alexis, not Agent Mills."

I grabbed the rope she was pointing to and handed it to her. "Okay." I smiled to myself. Alexis. It didn't feel right in my head. I liked last names, but I had earned her respect.

Alexis attached the rope to a pole on the edge of the rock wall. It was part of the safety net. She was dodging the question. Agent Mills finished attaching the rope and turned to me. She took a deep breath.

"The director left camp."

Chapter 28

The Big Man on Campus…is Gone

"Ms. Blanchard left?"

"That's why Agent Powell gave the announcement. He's the interim camp director."

Why would the director leave camp? Did it have something to do with that meeting? Agent Mills finished installing the safety net. I just stood there, watching, failing to put the pieces together.

"Where did she go?" I asked.

Agent Mills shook her head. "Not sure. She didn't even tell us she was leaving. Agent Powell said she left in the middle of the night after telling him he would have to take over for the rest of the summer." Agent Mills went quiet. I wanted one of her snarky comments to lighten the mood, but she said nothing. Ms. Blanchard left in the middle of the night without a single explanation. Why? Did we have our facts wrong?

"What are we supposed to do?" I asked. Alexis thought for a moment. Then she started laughing. "What's so funny?" This was not a time for laughter.

"We just wait," she said when her laughter subsided. Her smile felt like it was mocking me. What was so funny? "That's what Tanner always told me," she mumbled. "We just wait."

I figured this was an appropriate time to start questioning her sanity. "Well, we know Dr. Doom escaped. Maybe she went after him, or that stone. Maybe there was an emergency at Headquarters or something." There were a million possibilities. This wasn't a big deal. I couldn't let it become one. We just had to be patient, just wait until we knew more. Alexis brushed off my suggestions and kept smiling to herself. She tied up her last knot and set her gaze on me.

"I think I have a plan, but I have to make a phone call first."

"Why does that sound like a bad thing?" If there was one thing I learned about Agent Mills, once she put her mind to something, no one could talk her out of it. Any plan of hers was the one we were all expected to follow. All I could do was hope it was a good one.

Chapter 29

Conquering the Rock Wall

The rock wall loomed over me like a thunderstorm about to strike, the clouds enveloping you in a darkness so thick the wind blew away your thoughts. I stood at the base of the rock wall, the granite cold to the touch, its own shadow keeping the sun away. Why couldn't it be like one of those rock walls you could climb at the theme park, where it was a wall covered in plastic handholds. No, this was the T.S.O. This was the real world. And the real world was much more dangerous.

"Listen up!" Agent Mills shouted. She stood at the base of the mat with everyone standing around her. "To climb this wall takes three things." Her voice boomed to reach even those standing in the back. "What are they?"

A girl in the front raised her hand. "Strength?" Agent Mills nodded. A bit further back someone shouted "skill!"

"One more!" Agent Mills said. No one answered. "It takes focus! Strength, technique, and focus!" She turned in a slow circle to face those standing behind her. "Which one is the most important?" Alexis stopped and faced Oliss, who stood beside me. "Which one?"

Oliss stood up taller. "Focus."

Agent Mills nodded her approval. "Focus." She spoke louder again, facing the entire group. "If you can't stay focused, if you don't think about what you're doing, you *will* fall." I wondered if she was thinking about her own accident. Did she lose focus? Agent Mills looked back at Oliss and studied him for a moment. "It's Darwin, right?" Alexis asked.

"Yes." I couldn't tell what Oliss was thinking, but the furrow in his brow said he wasn't happy. "Oliss Darwin."

"Good job." Oliss shifted his weight and looked away from Agent Mills. She pursed her lips. "Who wants to go first?"

This time, I volunteered.

We were strapped to harnesses and smothered our hands in chalk. Four people at a time. Footing was everything. Focus was the most important. After a quick instruction, I grabbed hold of the rock. As gently as possible, I gripped the rock with my foot. I stared at the spot where my hands would rest and slowly made my way up the wall.

Imagining Agent Mills doing this without a harness kept me going. If she got hurt like that and came back years later to face her fears like a true hero, then I could do this no problem. My muscles tensed as I pulled myself up. The safety net crept its way up the wall right below the slowest of us. If I fell, it wouldn't be all the way back to the ground.

I made the mistake of looking down a quarter up. My foot slipped. I grabbed onto the wall to steady myself and caught my balance. Focus. I couldn't lose focus. I had the strength. That's all I had been working on since I got here. I needed to believe in myself.

After ten minutes of climbing, I made it halfway to where the marker was. The markers were placed halfway up the wall. We weren't allowed to go higher yet. I glanced at the climbers on either side of me. Two were almost at the markers, a good five feet above me. One guy was just below me on my left.

I grunted, grabbing onto the wall as I climbed higher. The other agents-in-training reached the end. Some people clapped from below us. Because of the net, they had to wait for the last person to get to the top before they could repel down.

After another minute of carefully placing my feet and hauling myself up, I made it. Relief flooded my system as I hugged the rock. I clung to it, frozen, feeling my breath steady. My muscles pulled at the strain. My head leaned against the rock, a smile playing at my lips. A minute later the final climber made it. Another round of clapping echoed up the rock wall as I used the harness for support and bounced my way back down with the other climbers, the net following our descent.

"Well done." Agent Mills helped me out of my harness and I stepped off the mat. That wasn't so bad.

Oliss took my place, and I watched him climb.

Chapter 30

When the Instructors Are Worried, Everyone is Worried

By the end of the day everyone had taken a turn on the rock wall. A handful of people fell, but the net caught all of them before they could get hurt. It was announced that campers could train on the wall during their free time with instructor supervision. Now everyone was preparing for the obstacle course, which would be at the end of the week. Every day was spent preparing, trying to figure out what we would need to succeed. One night, Oliss explained that the obstacle course had three focuses: strength, intelligence, and teamwork. There would be a winning cabin and a single winner for best performance. I didn't need to win. I just needed to prove I could do it.

I stared at the bunk on top of me, letting the darkness carry my thoughts. Now Ms. Blanchard wasn't here. Agent Powell was in charge. Was she going to come back? I imagined my foot slipping on the wall, and I watched myself fall into the safety net below. The T.S.O. stood for strength of mind, body, and soul. Did I really have what it takes?

After two weeks of training with Agent Mills, I didn't feel ready.

The next morning, Agent Mills didn't show up for our morning training. I trained on my own, failing to make sense of the information inside my head. When it was time for breakfast, I met cabin eleven at our table. None of the instructors were there.

"Where is everybody?" I asked. Did they all disappear like Ms. Blanchard?

Before someone could answer me, the cafeteria doors flew open. Agent P.R. stormed inside, grabbed a plate of food, and sat at the instructors' table. Agent Powell and Agent Willow followed, with Agent Mills and the others in tow. They were talking amongst themselves. Agent Mills looked quiet. That wasn't a good sign.

"What's wrong?" Oliss asked, leaning closer to us. Nobody at the table answered. All the oxygen was sucked out of the room.

I thought things were going okay. Other than Ms. Blanchard disappearing, I was making progress. Campers were learning. What was making everyone so upset? Agent Powell And Agent X argued in hushed tones.

"It's like they were all told they were fired or something," Handel whispered. Kids were starting to talk at other tables, wondering what made all the instructors agitated.

"Class won't be easy today, will it?" Ethan asked.

I needed an excuse to get out of class. Field Operations was a cool class. Every day our instructor, Agent X, would give us a mission and the class would go through different scenarios as if we were in the field on a case. I usually enjoyed it, but not today. It was my third class of the day, and I couldn't sit still.

Today's mission involved tracking through enemy territory in the woods to scout out the enemy's base. So far, we had come up with a way to blend into the environment using camouflage and having teammates scout ahead for spies. The only problem was no one mentioned the trees possibly being rigged by the enemy. Agent X always threw some unknown variable into her missions.

There were too many unknown variables now. Agent Mills said she wanted my help. She said she had a plan, and that was the last I spoke to her. The rock wall training was three days ago. She hadn't shown up for morning practice since then. What was it we were missing from the equation? What roles did Amelia and Emily play? All the instructors were on edge. Agent X looked just as distracted as I was. I had to get out of the classroom. I had to find Agent Mills.

My hand shot into the air. "Agent X?"

"Yes?"

"I don't feel so good." The one perk about having a dad who didn't pay any attention to you. You got really good at faking being sick. "I think I need a doctor." My voice shook.

"You do look a little pale. Okay." Agent X nodded her head. It was probably a good thing she was distracted, because I wasn't trying very hard. "Go see Dr. Powell. I'll tell him you're on your way."

I hobbled out of the classroom and staggered down the stairs. When the door closed, I dashed across the field towards the infirmary. I had to check in now since Agent X was going to contact him. A headache and some stomach nausea would do fine. I could blame it on the food and say I felt fine now.

I pushed the door open and stepped inside the mini hospital to the sound of raised voices.

"You can't do that!" Agent Mills shouted. The door to the hallway was open. Tiptoeing, I headed down the hall, following the voices into Dr. Powell's Office.

Dr. Powell stood behind his desk. He leaned forward on his desk, his hands propping him up as he listened to Agent Mills. When was the last time he slept? There were bags under his eyes, and his shirt was wrinkled. Agent Mills had her back to me. She shook her head, her leather jacket moving with her shoulders.

"It's not my call." Agent Powell shook his head. They hadn't seen me. I cleared my throat. They both shot me a look.

"Tony, what are you doing here?" Agent Mills asked. She was furious.

"Looking for you," I said. "What is going on?"

Agent Powell sighed. "Don't tell me you've brought in a camper," he said.

"He's friends with Agent Z and Steinfeld," Agent Mills said.

"Oh." Agent Powell adjusted his white doctor's coat. "I see."

"What is going on?" I asked. It was getting harder to hold back my tongue. We were part of the T.S.O. too. It wasn't fair for the instructors to hold back information, not when we were involved.

Agent Mills pulled on her fingerless gloves and stepped forward. "We were right."

"Right about what?"

"The T.S.O. is being threatened to go public."

"They can't do that," I said. I wasn't even an agent yet, but I understood the need to be secret. Teenagers willingly confronting dangerous people and putting their lives at risk was not something the public would agree with. It would make our jobs a whole lot harder if the world knew about the Teen Spy Organization.

"We didn't," Agent Powell said. "There was an anonymous tip given to the press about an underground agency of teenage spies."

"Wait, so do people know about the T.S.O. or not?"

"It sounds like people are taking it as a rumor, but we're not sure." Agent Powell shook his head.

"But Mr. Martial wants to go public," Agent Mills said. "And some other people in the T.S.O. One of them could have easily given a tip to the press. They might take this as their chance to tell the world about us. Who knows how many secrets have already been divulged."

"Is that why Ms. Blanchard left?" I asked.

Agent Powell nodded. "That and some other problems at Headquarters. I've been warned we might have to cut camp short."

"Agent Powell, you can't do that," Agent Mills pleaded. This was why all the instructors were upset at breakfast, and why Agent Mills didn't show up for training. "The only way to fight this is to keep training agents. Shutting down camp weakens the entire agency. What does that show all of these trainees? When things get hard, give up? We could lose their trust and their secrecy. If the public really finds out we exist, we're all in danger of getting shut down. We can't show our own people that we're afraid."

"I agree," I said. I'd come too far to be sent home. I couldn't quit. There was almost a month left of camp. If my dad found out about the T.S.O., I would never be allowed to be a part of it. If I came home earlier than expected, he would never let me go to camp again. He acted like kids couldn't do anything but be annoying. I had to show him he was wrong. "I'm not leaving camp."

"No one wants to shut down the camp," Agent Powell said. "But if things get worse, and I'm given the order, I won't have a choice."

Chapter 31

Time to Step Up

I wanted to tell my cabin. I wanted to tell everyone. Shouldn't everyone know about this? If the very thing we were all here for was at risk, we had a right to know. At the same time, I understood not wanting to worry anyone. There was a problem at Headquarters where my friends were, and they didn't even know I was a part of this. It wasn't fair.

The next morning, Alexis made an appearance at our pre-breakfast training. She was angrier than I could have imagined. And that's saying a lot. The scenario with the rubber gun from my first day of camp was like a memory stabbing me in the brain.

"This is all my fault," she said, throwing a punch that took everything in me to avoid.

"What is?"

Agent Mills stopped sparring and sighed. She balled her fists. "Everything," she said. "Mr. Bard said he would do this, and I didn't listen." She started pacing on the mat. "It was him, Tony. I know it. This is Mr. Bard's doing. Mr.

Martial is too much of a pussy to pull something like this. Not by himself."

"Then it's his fault, not yours," I said.

Agent Mills shook her head. "I pushed it too far. I should have just let Watson have that case. Mr. Bard knows about the T.S.O. He's got to be the one who told the press, and he will exploit everything if we don't do what he wants. He has too much power."

"What do you think he wants?" I asked.

"I'm not sure." It didn't really matter though. He was the bad guy. We couldn't give him what he wanted. We had to keep working towards what was right. "Well," Agent Mills started. "We have to be ready. I've called my friends. They will be coming here if anything else happens. Apparently, things aren't good back in Ohio."

"How so?"

"We have to prepare for the worst. If camp shuts down, we can't go back home. It will be too dangerous. We'll be too exposed. We'll have to figure something out before it's too late."

I nodded. I wanted to help. If only to show my dad that I was capable of something important. He would be pissed if I showed up at home, before the end of camp, and ruined his schedule. "I need to fight better," I said.

Agent Mills looked at me. "What?"

"My training. We need to step it up." If I was going to be of any help, I had to be ready for a fight, right? I couldn't hold her back, or anyone else. With the obstacle course in a few days, I wanted to be ready.

"Now you're talking like an agent." Agent Mills turned toward me, and the fight was on.

Keeping a secret wasn't easy. I didn't know who I could trust, even at camp. During our free period our cabin got together to discuss our strategy for the competition. As Oliss talked, I remembered the look Agent Mills gave him at the Rock Wall. Maybe I could call Amelia or Emily. They would know more about what's going on. They had to. If only I had a phone, or a computer. Was snagging a phone from an instructor an option? Of course, stealing from an agent sounded like a bad idea.

"Alright," Oliss continued. We sat on the dock, out of earshot. Ethan swung his legs over the water, Handel and I perched next to him. "The competition is a relay race. We need to decide who does which part and inform the instructors."

Everyone nodded in agreement. I had been thinking about the obstacle course all night, along with everything else that had happened. This was my chance to prove myself.

"There are five parts," Oliss said. "One for each of us. Part one is the wall."

"What's the wall?" Handel asked.

"It's a wall," Oliss said. "You have to scale the wall while holding the baton. It's about ten feet high. That's Bentley's part." Bentley nodded. He was strong and agile. He could tackle the wall, no problem.

"What's part two?" Ethan asked, waving his legs and leaning towards the water.

"Part two is the mind game. Tony, that's yours." Oliss pointed at me. "It's like a maze, with a bunch of traps that require a lot of technical or mental strategy to get out."

It sounded cool, but I wanted to fight. "Why can't I do the combat portion?" I asked. I needed to test myself after all of my training.

"Your greatest skill set is in the mind game," Oliss said. "That's where we need you."

"He's right," Handel said. I sighed. Wasn't the point of this to challenge us? Why would I do the one part everyone said I was good at? I didn't argue though. Oliss was too set to change his game plan.

The next level was the rock wall. You had to make it to the top then climb down a net which would be fastened on the other side. Handel was in charge of that part since he scaled the rock wall faster than any of us during practice. Oliss ended up with the combat portion, where he would have to get past his opponent without losing the baton. The very last level was Ethan's. After Oliss would hand him the baton, he had a mile run to the finish line. And since Ethan was the fastest, it was perfect for him.

Chapter 32

Into the Woods We Go

The next day was spent preparing. We had submitted our assignments for the competition, and now we waited. I sparred with Oliss, and we timed Ethan on the track. He could run a mile in six minutes. Handel practiced on the rock wall and Oliss explained the mind game to me. He had done it last year, and his team lost. Oliss said the best way to win was to have everyone at their top strength, where they excel the most. I guess it made sense.

"So, the mind game is a maze?" I asked.

"More or less." Oliss said. "When you start, you will be handed a backpack. There is a table full of gadgets. You can take as many as you can carry with the baton. The maze is different every year, so I don't know what you should expect."

"So, I'm going in blind with a backpack of gadgets?" Now I sounded like Emily and her *Backpack of Everything* that she always carried around with her.

"Pretty much." Oliss shrugged his shoulders like it was no big deal. "There are a lot of places in there where you can't move forward without solving a puzzle or something. There are different challenges that you have to complete, like a virtual mission or escaping from a trap. Things like that."

"Sounds easy enough," I said. Getting myself into trouble was my specialty, but so was using my wits to solve problems.

"It's more difficult than you think," Oliss said. "Remember how they said at camp they will make us expand our limits?" I nodded, not sure where this was going. "Well, that's what this does. It plays with your emotions. I'm not sure how else to explain it. It's different for every competitor."

"I think I can handle it," I said.

After dinner we all headed straight to bed. The competition started after breakfast. There was a nervous pit bull running around in my stomach, and I needed to sleep. Everything about the T.S.O. going public, about the director, about my friends and Dr. Doom; I pushed it all aside. Those things could wait. Tomorrow was the obstacle course. Three weeks left of classes before final exams, then we would be done. Right now, the obstacle course took priority over everything else. I wanted to fight, simply to prove to myself that I could. And now I wouldn't have the chance to on the course.

Final exams were like another competition, one for each class. Maybe that would be the time to prove myself. I had to be ready for anything.

The competition course was set up in the woods. We hiked through the trees until every sign of the camp was gone. Birds called out as we headed down the trail. Excitement rose in my chest with every step. Sure, I wouldn't get to be in hand-to-hand combat, but at least I wouldn't make a fool of myself losing a fight to someone.

The trees loomed above us, their blankets of leaves leaving gaps where the sunlight peeked through.

We kept walking. Were they trying to tire us out before we even started? At this point I wouldn't be surprised.

Each cabin would be graded based on their time of completion. The cabin that finishes first wins.

When we finally arrived at the course, Bentley took his position and was given our team's baton. The rest of us kept walking to the next point. A little way further in the trees would be my challenge. The trees thinned out before giving away completely to a small clearing. A grey wall towered over us, its shadow waiting to snuff out the sunlight.

"This is it," Oliss said. He patted me on the shoulder. I watched as the rest of my cabin and all the other campers disappeared back into the trees and onto their next stop. There were eleven other kids, six girls and five boys, one from each cabin. We gawked at the enormous entrance in front of us.

Agent P.R. stepped in front of us "Alright, this is how this works." The entrance to the maze was like a giant doorway that seemed to stop only when it touched the sky. We stepped up to him. On each side of our instructor, two tables were set up against the cement wall. "You choose a backpack, then you fill it." Agent P.R. pointed to the backpacks under the tables. "When your teammate arrives, you have to wait until they hand you the baton to enter the mind game."

Down at my feet was a yellow strip of tape. "You are not allowed to pass this line until the baton is in your hand," Agent P.R. explained.

"Inside there are a series of challenges you have to face to continue. When you get out, follow the trail until you get to the rock wall. There you will hand off the baton to your next teammate. You may begin."

I grabbed a backpack from under the table on the left and examined everything on top. There could be any kind of obstacle in the maze. I had to be ready for anything. I grabbed a key card, a grappling hook pen, an acid pen, night vision goggles, a mini crowbar, and a few other things. Nothing I grabbed was heavy, so it shouldn't slow me down. When I was done, I stood at the yellow tape, waiting.

I shifted my weight from foot to foot. The backpack felt heavier on my shoulders as I waited. A few minutes later, a bustling sound came from the trees in front of us. A girl came running through the foliage, a baton held tightly in her grasp. I perked up, adjusting the backpack. Bentley came flying through the forest next, our baton grasped in his fingers. I stepped up to the yellow line anxious to get moving.

"Here!" Bentley shoved the baton in my hands, huffing out the single word. I grabbed it so hard my nails dug into my skin, then turned towards the opening in the cement wall and entered the mind game.

Chapter 33

The Mind Game

Immediately, I was faced with a choice. In front of me were three paths, one to the left, one to my right, the other straight ahead. I could see the girl who entered before me running down the tunnel in front of me. You would think it was the fastest way, but that would be too obvious. I headed into the tunnel on my right.

After running a few yards down the tunnel, the light disappeared. A ceiling stretched out on top, blocking out the hot rays of the sun. Slipping the backpack off my shoulders, I grabbed the night vision goggles and tucked the baton inside the bag. With the ability to see in shades of green, I continued down the tunnel. The dark made everything feel creepy. I turned in a circle. Nothing was behind me, but I knew I was being watched. There had to be cameras somewhere.

At the end of the tunnel was a wall. Bright flashes of light messed with my vision. I pulled off the night vision goggles.

A lightbulb swung from the ceiling. The wall wasn't just a wall. There were elevator doors, shining in the dim light. But what confused me was the table standing in front of it. A metal table with a metal chair in front of me. Stepping closer, I could see the tablet attached to the table, propped up so whoever sat in the chair could clearly see the screen. **SIT DOWN**, the screen read.

My heart thumped in my chest. It was my first challenge. I could do this. I just had to figure out how to open the doors.

There was no way I was sitting in that chair. I walked around the table. There wasn't anything odd about it, other than the fact that it was here in the first place. It was like an interrogation room set up in the middle of the maze, the dirt providing a soft ground to confess on. The dirt. Around the chair there was no dirt. I bent down and looked closer. The chair was surrounded by a metal slab of concrete. Nope, definitely not sitting there.

I tapped the screen on the tablet. Nothing changed. I had to sit down for anything to happen. This did not look good. Instead of sitting down and possibly getting trapped, I slipped off the backpack and looked inside.

"Here we go." I pulled out the mini crowbar, the heaviest thing I brought with me, and set it on the chair.

A glass cylinder shot down from the ceiling, encasing the chair. I jumped back, tripping over the backpack as I dropped it. My breath was quick now. The tablet's screen flickered. I grabbed the backpack off the ground and peered at the tablet.

"Tony." It was Zegro's voice. She was sitting on the hospital bed, exactly how I saw her the last time she was in there. She looked exhausted, her eyes fighting to stay open. Was she back in the hospital? I couldn't breathe. Was this a real video? Or was it just a fake created for this very moment? "Tony, I need to ask you something."

131

I couldn't help it. I grabbed the rim of the table, leaning closer to the screen. "Amelia?" My heart rate quickened at the sight of her. She looked like she was in so much pain, and there was nothing I could do to help her.

"Do you remember when you pranked Emily with the whipped cream?" she asked.

I nodded my head. That felt like forever ago.

"Are you okay?" I asked.

Amelia laughed and winced. "She was so angry at you." I stared at the screen. What happened to her? I had to help her, had to do something. Did Dr. Doom get to her again? But I was stuck at the end of this tunnel in the middle of the weirdest obstacle course I'd ever been in. "She forgave you though," Amelia sighed. "Listen, when I get out of here, we should all go to the mall or something." Amelia rambled on about a shopping trip.

I stepped away from the table as her scratchy, sore voice kept going. Something wasn't right. Amelia hated shopping, and she hardly ever talked so much about something so unimportant. This wasn't her. It couldn't be. Now that I realized it, her eyes didn't follow me as I stepped around the table. It was just a video. And I was supposed to be stuck in the chair, forced to watch it. I had to get out of here.

Chapter 34

Push the Button

The doors wouldn't budge, and I couldn't reach the light. Amelia was still talking, but I wasn't listening anymore. It couldn't be real. And if it was, she really needed help. I wasn't any use to her if I was stuck in here. I looked back at the chair, where I was supposed to be sitting. On the back of the chair was a red button. Something you wouldn't be able to see if you were sitting in it let alone reach in that tiny space. It had to open the doors. But now I had a new problem. I was on the wrong side of the glass.

"Seriously?" I sighed. Then I remembered the backpack full of gadgets. I pulled out the acid pen. Perfect. Drawing the worst circle ever, the glass melted and separated under the touch of the acid. Only a few acids could eat away at glass, so this was powerful stuff. The awful circle gave way and fell.

"Don't leave me alone," Amelia's voice said from the tablet.

I froze for a moment, listening to the panic in her voice. But it wasn't real. It sounded so real. I sighed. "I'll never leave you alone," I said, and I pushed the button.

I did it. The video stopped. **Congratulations** flashed across the screen. The elevator doors slid open. Relief filled my spirits. I shook my head and smiled, grabbing the backpack and running through the doors.

The ceiling was gone, so the light of the sun felt almost blinding compared to the darkness I came from. A little way ahead I was faced with another fork in the road. I stayed to the right. If I kept to the walls as best as possible, maybe I wouldn't get lost. The next challenge came shortly after.

Once again elevator-like doors blocked the path. This time a large screen hung on the left side of the tunnel. A button with the word **Begin** flashed at the bottom of the screen. Psyching myself up, I pushed the button.

This time it was easy. It was just like Logistical Tactics. A scenario played in front of me. Someone being held in the basement of a house needed to be rescued. It was a multiple-choice answer, one after another, that moved the game forward. The victim was saved and the doors opened in no time.

I ran down the tunnel with more energy. The last challenge was easy. But the sight of Amelia in so much pain kept me from feeling too confident. I still had to get out of this place and get the baton to Handel.

Two more turns and three mind games later, I felt like I was almost at the finish. I came to a stop at another elevator door. But there was nothing there. I searched the walls for some sort of clue or game. Next to the elevator was a small keyhole. The key card. I pulled it out of my bag and jammed it into the lock. The doors slid open.

I stepped through, coming to a stop. I was confused. I ran straight ahead, wondering if it was an illusion. There was a brick wall in front of me, and on all sides. It was a dead end. I turned back towards the elevator doors. They slid shut.

"No!" I shouted. I pounded my fist against the door and searched for a keyhole. But there was nothing there. I was trapped.

This had to be some sort of test. Everything in here was a test. The sun beat down on my face from above. The walls were too tall and too smooth to climb out. I ran my fingers along the wall and walked around the small room. My hand grazed along the walls, my eyes searching for anything out of the ordinary. There it was.

As my hand moved along the wall, towards the end of the room my hand hit nothing. There was an illusion hiding an indent in the wall, a hidden passageway. I smiled to myself and slipped in between the brick. It opened up to another hallway, this time with a ceiling. A small line of lights ran across the middle of the ceiling, and I ran down the pathway. How long had I been in there? Twenty minutes? Had the others already finished? The last trap had me wondering if I could make it out in time. I couldn't be the last one. That would just be embarrassing. I ran with a smile on my face, hoping I was about to make it out. That is, until I reached the next set of doors.

Chapter 35

My Father, My Nightmare

I was starting to understand why it was called the mind game.

"Dad." I skidded to a stop, goosebumps running down my arms. He stood in front of the elevator door, his arms crossed, eyes narrowed as he looked down his nose. He was in his usual business suit, with his nice shoes that he claims were too cheap for his job as an accountant. "What are you doing here?" I asked.

"What did you do this time?" he scolded. His voice was dripping with anger.

"What do you mean? I didn't do anything!" This had to be another trick. The T.S.O. had a sick way of training people if they used their own mind against them. Or maybe they were just that smart, trying to erase all forms of weakness.

"I can't believe you, Tony!" His arms flew around him as he yelled. "I thought we were done with the lying and the games."

"What are you talking about?" I studied my father. His image flickered. It was a hologram. My father was just a hologram. I waved my hand through his stomach. He wasn't really here. Despite his very realistic lecture, I smiled. This was kind of cool. On the grass below my father's feet was a disk, almost like a DVD. That had to be what was projecting the hologram.

"You have to stop pulling these things, Tony," Dad continued. "First you keep running off to hang out with your friends, and now you lie to me about camp and take off for the summer!"

I didn't answer. I knelt down at my dad's feet and tried to pull at the holographic device. It wouldn't move.

"Answer me, Tony!" I jumped back to my feet. It was so real. Why would the T.S.O. rig a hologram of my dad? He was in his element, when he yelled at me about all his problems and claimed my shenanigans were the reason for his issues at work. "I had to leave a meeting for this!" he shouted. Hence my point.

I opened my mouth to say something, but the words caught my throat. I've had this conversation with him before. It felt so real.

"Dad, I'm sorry." Obviously, I couldn't just turn off the hologram. There had to be another way to shut it off. Maybe if I played along with the conversation. "Listen, this camp is awesome! I've learned so much," I said.

"It doesn't matter. You still lied to me." He actually responded. Maybe it wasn't as fake as I thought.

I gulped. How were they doing this? "Last time I checked you were all over me going to camp. You wanted me out of the way so you could work all summer."

"I never said that." His eyes flickered. Was it actually him, somehow being live streamed from a different place? The T.S.O. wouldn't do that just for a test, would they? Ms.

Blanchard said parents were not always informed about the T.S.O.

"You didn't have to." I grabbed onto the backpack strap until my knuckles hurt. "All I want is to make you proud. And every time I try to do something with you, you blow me off. You blame me for all your problems. Ever since Mom left, you've done nothing but push me away."

I tried to let the words sink in. The memory burned in my brain. A few years ago, she left without a word to either of us. I was so angry at her, not for leaving me, but for leaving Dad. It broke his heart, and he acted like it was my fault so much that I started to believe it. Maybe that's why I was always pranking my friends and didn't care about being responsible. Dad always said I messed things up and couldn't take anything seriously, so I started to act that way. I wasn't proud of it, but the T.S.O. was helping me change that.

Dad looked taken aback, which was impressive for a hologram. "I'm sorry," he said. "I am proud of you, son." As much as I wanted the words to ring true, I knew they didn't. This was just a programmed conversation. Someone else was controlling his responses back at camp. "I didn't realize I was pushing you away. I don't want that," he said.

"You spend so much time working, you hardly come home for dinner. You never talk to me other than to yell at me for making you upset." Why was I so upset? It's just a hologram. Tony! Snap out of it!

"This is a cool camp," Dad said. He turned his head from side to side, like he was admiring the dank walls that surrounded us. "When you get home, things will be different. I promise."

I nodded, unsure what exactly was going on. "That would be nice," I said.

Then my father disappeared. In a flash of light, he was gone, the disk lying on the ground. The elevator doors slid open. I dashed through them before they could open all the way.

Chapter 36

And the Winner is...

I kept running. There were no more doors. The exit was in front of me. Running faster, I burst through the exit and skidded to a stop. Looking back inside the mind game, I saw three tunnels, just like the entrance to the maze. I had come out of the left tunnel, on the opposite side to where I started. Another camper emerged from the tunnel behind me.

The conversation with my hologram dad stung as I ran across the grass and into the trees, following the trail outlined by yellow tape.

The rock wall came into view. How long was I in the mind game? I ran faster. I couldn't be the last one out. The sound of someone's footsteps behind me urged me to run faster. Oliss would be furious if I was the reason we came in last. When I arrived at the rock wall, a flood of relief washed over me, pushing me forward. All twelve competitors were there. I was the first one out of the maze!

I slipped the backpack off and ran the last couple yards with it in my hands. Handel would have to climb the rock wall and down a net that was on the other side. He couldn't do that with a baton in his hand, not easily.

Handel was already fastened to a harness, standing at the edge of the safety mat, waiting for me. "It's inside!" I wheezed, shoving the backpack through his arms. The thought of Agent Mills' accident left a lump in my throat as Handel began his climb. The image of Amelia in the hospital almost made me lose my balance. Handel could do this. I watched him scale up the wall with ease, one hand after another, his feet choosing their perches carefully.

When Handel was a quarter of the way up, a girl came crashing through the trees behind me. It was the girl who had entered the mind game before me. Her backpack was gone. She handed the baton to her teammate, who started climbing. The girl put her hands on her knees and caught her breath. I think she was holding back tears.

Three minutes later two more kids ran through the woods. Handel was almost to the top of the wall. Not long after, the rest of the people who entered the maze came running down the trail towards the rock wall. By the time the last competitor arrived, Handel had taken off his harness and began descending the net on the opposite side.

"You kids come with me." It was the man who signed me in when I first arrived. He directed us to a golf cart that was towing a mini trailer, fastened with a bench along the side. "Hop in. We're going to the finish line."

The twelve of us mind game participants climbed into the trailer and were off.

The cart took us to the edge of the woods where the trees gave way to the lake. We hopped off the trailer. I found Bentley and the rest of the kids from the first level of the obstacle course. A yellow strip of tape was attached to two trees. The finish line was waiting to be broken. We still had to wait for Handel to get the baton to Oliss, then to Ethan.

The backpack was a good idea, considering Oliss would have to fight an opponent with the baton.

"How did it go?" I asked.

Bentley nodded his head. "Easy. You?"

"That was a trip." I thought about all the challenges I had to face. The first game and the last messed with my head, but the rest were rather easy. The maze was not something I would do again by choice.

A few minutes later a supervising agent announced the first competitors had completed the rock wall and were off to the next level. Bentley and I didn't say much else. I couldn't stand still. The golf cart returned with the competitors from level three.

"Hey!" Handel waved to us and hopped off the trailer.

"How did you do?" I asked as he joined us.

"I finished first." His smile reached his ears. I raised my hand for a high five.

About ten minutes later the same agent announced that the first competitor had started the mile run. That meant someone already completed the one-on-one combat. We could only hope it was Ethan running the last leg of the race.

Another ten minutes passed. My feet ached as I shifted my weight. Before I lost my sanity from impatience, a girl came running through the woods towards the finish line. Part of me was excited, the other part was disappointed. I looked at Bentley and he shrugged his shoulders. "Come on," Handel said, wringing his hands together.

Ethan emerged from around a bend of trees. He was gaining distance, fast. The backpack bounced in beat with his footsteps. I had never seen someone run so fast.

But he wasn't fast enough. Right before Ethan could pass the girl, she tore through the yellow tape. Ethan ran through the trees a few feet behind her. We came in second.

Ethan and the girl ran to a stop ahead of us and came back to meet us. The girl had the biggest smile on her face. I couldn't blame her. Ethan was smiling too, but he was always smiling.

"Nice job!" Handel slapped Ethan on the back. The four of us exchanged high fives. Second wasn't bad. Two more people emerged from the woods. We turned in the baton and the golf cart delivered the competitors from level four. Oliss staggered towards us. He looked exhausted.

"How did we do?" he asked, trying to hide his panting.

"Second place," Handel said.

Oliss nodded. "Not bad." After knowing what I had to go through, I wasn't disappointed either. "I had to fight Mills," Oliss said. He was holding his side. Agent Mills probably kicked him in the ribs. "I couldn't get past her."

A second golf cart wheeled towards us filled with instructors. Agent Mills was one of them.

"Attention everyone!"

We turned towards a table set up near the trees. Agent Powell stood in front of it. "Congratulations, everyone! You finished the team obstacle course!" An eruption of cheers and clapping filled the small clearing. "Coming in third place we have cabin nine." A group of guys stepped up to the table. They were each given a white ribbon. "In second place we have cabin eleven." Ethan gave a whoop and we made our way to the table. Agent Powell handed each of us a red ribbon. T.S.O. was written on it in gold letters. **Level 2, Mind Game** was stitched onto mine. When I looked up, I caught Agent Mills smiling at us. "In first place we have cabin two." The girls from cabin two received their blue ribbons with smiles.

When everyone quieted, we headed to the cafeteria for lunch. The rest of today's classes were canceled so everyone could celebrate. Unfortunately, that was the last of the good news we would receive today.

143

Chapter 37

Bad News and Burgers

Everyone crowded into the cafeteria. Burgers and hot dogs were being served. I slathered ketchup on my burger and took a seat at our table.

"That was crazy!" Ethan said.

"How long were you running?" Handel asked.

"Six, maybe seven minutes. That girl started a while before me, but I caught up to her, almost."

Oliss huffed. "Agent Mills is hard to fight. She stole the backpack from me twice." That was easy to believe. "How was the mind game?"

I stared at my burger. "Challenging." How was I supposed to describe it? I didn't want to tell them about Amelia and my dad. That would just be weird. Before I could say anything else, Dr. Powell called for everyone's attention.

"First off, congratulations again, everyone." Cheers erupted from the tables. Dr. Powell frowned. *Please, no. Don't say it.* "Unfortunately, I have some bad news." Of course, he does. My head dropped. I lost my appetite. The clapping stopped. When everyone was quiet, Agent Powell continued. I knew what he was going to say before he made a sound. "I'm afraid to say that camp will be cut short. At the end of the week, you will all be sent home."

"What?" Oliss asked. My heart sank. Whatever they were fearing, whatever order Dr. Powell was waiting for, it came. It happened.

"So," Dr. Powell continued. "We will finish off the week in celebration." His attempt to make the announcement seem less severe didn't work. Everybody was talking to the point where I couldn't tell if my thoughts were mine or someone else's. They were going to shut down camp at the end of the week. Sending everyone home early wasn't going to send a good message. I couldn't go home early. Dad would be angrier than his hologram. No one should have to leave. This was wrong.

Chapter 38

Never Mind. It Can Always Get Worse.

I wasn't hungry anymore. The food in my stomach felt flat. Among the chaos of angry campers, I spotted Agent Mills rushing out the cafeteria doors. I jumped from my seat and ran after her.

"Hey!" I shouted. I ran towards her, but she didn't slow down. She continued across the field. "Agent Mills!"

"Not now, Tony!" She waved a hand at me and kept walking. There was no way she was going to shut me out now.

I ran towards Agent Mills until I was in front of her. "What just happened in there?" I asked, forcing her to stop walking away.

Agent Mills sighed and crossed her arms, glaring at me. I didn't budge. She looked around the field, making sure no one was around. "After Ms. Blanchard said to shut down camp, we lost all contact with Headquarters."

I didn't know what that meant. Did the director just choose to go silent? Was she really trying to make the T.S.O. go public after all? People could already know about the

Teen Spy Organization, and we wouldn't even know because we aren't allowed to have contact with anyone outside camp.

Agent Mills glared at me. "Tony, Headquarters has been attacked."

"Attacked? Do you mean someone broke into headquarters?"

"Yes. Just a couple hours ago. We just found out."

I tried to process this, but the gears in my brain were jammed. The T.S.O. was attacked? So, did it already go public? I couldn't move. I was starting to understand why everyone wasn't told about this. People would freak out. And closing the camp would keep everyone safer, hopefully. But what was safer than a secret organization's camp for agents-in-training? What was safer than the T.S.O. Headquarters?

"Who broke into Headquarters?" I asked.

If I hadn't known Agent Mills and her way of always looking scary, I would have been a three-year-old in preschool having an accident. All the color drained from her face. She looked at me like I asked the worst possible question in the history of ever.

"Dr. Doom," she said.

"Doom? He broke into Headquarters?"

"And we think he has hostages."

Chapter 39

Runaway Campers

I sat against a tree at the edge of the woods, not sure how much time had passed. It was hard to take a full breath. The man who injured one of my best friends had not only escaped jail, but had infiltrated the T.S.O. I had a feeling it was almost as secure as the White House, if not more. Who knows what could be happening there right now? If all contact was silent with Headquarters, how would we know if people were in there? There had to be, which meant everyone inside Headquarters was in danger.

Why would Dr. Doom even break into Headquarters? From what I knew, the only person he could really hold a grudge against would be Amelia, and maybe his niece, Savannah. I didn't know her well from school. She never talked to anyone. But Amelia was an agent. She could be a hostage right now, stuck inside Headquarters with a mad man.

"See you soon." Agent Mills hung up the phone and came out of the woods. "My friends will be here by tonight."

"What are they going to do?" I knew Agent Mills had been forming a plan, but I hadn't known any of the details.

"The T.S.O. is in danger," she said.

I rolled my eyes. "I thought that much was obvious."

"I can't go back to Ohio. Mr. Martial will have everyone on lockdown. I'm not even sure what side he's on. The best way to fix this is to go where the problem started."

"You mean Headquarters?" I laughed. "And how do you propose we do that? Besides, I'm an awful fighter."

Agent Mills sighed, throwing her arms in the air. "Tony, there is more to being an agent than being able to fight!" She shook her head at me. "Listen, when my friends get here, we're heading to a safehouse until we know what to do. If you go home, you can't do anything to help. I doubt they'll contact anybody who isn't a full agent until everything has calmed down. By then it will be too late to save your friends. So, the only way to do something about this whole mess is to come with me."

"You want me to run away from camp?" I stood up and brushed the dirt from my pants.

"You have until tonight to decide." With that, Agent Mills left.

Chapter 40

Doors Can't Stop Me

I had to call Amelia. I had to know she was okay before I made a decision. Knots formed at the base of my throat just thinking about what could be happening to her. The video from the mind game didn't help. Since classes were canceled, all the classrooms were empty. It was my only chance to get my hands on a phone since Agent Mills refused to let me borrow hers.

I rushed across the lawn to the gadgetry classroom. What was I supposed to do? I didn't want to go with Agent Mills on some quest. It was too dangerous. But staying at camp and getting sent home didn't seem right either. I had to know what Amelia thought. I had to know she was okay.

The door was unlocked. It was still light outside, the sunrays seeping through the upturned blinds. I scanned the table of gadgets set up in the front of the room. There was no cell phone. All the desks were empty. There had to be something. I sighed.

"What am I supposed to do?" My voice carried over the empty tables.

There was a door to my right, hidden by a sliding whiteboard. I rushed to it, pushed the whiteboard out of the way, and shook the door handle. It was locked.

I ran back to the table, picked up a key card, and jammed it into the door lock. They couldn't expect agents-in-training to not go exploring, right? After all, they taught us how to break into places.

I smiled as the door opened. It was a small storage room. Boxes lined the shelves on every wall. They were all labeled. Outdoor equipment, obstacle course gadgets, night vision goggles. I opened the box. It was filled with the same glasses we learned about in class. There were tons of boxes, each labeled with something different. I skimmed the shelves. Something here had to be useful. Then I spotted it. A box labeled with **phones** sat on the bottom shelf. I pulled it out.

The cardboard box had two cases inside. One had flip phones, the other smartphones. Of course, in a place like this every tool was probably being traced. I pulled out an old flip phone. Maybe it would be harder to track a phone call since it was an older model. I punched in Amelia's number.

I waited and waited. I could feel every moment ticking away that her voice didn't connect on the other line. Voicemail. I didn't know if that was good or bad. I deleted the call from the phone's history, shut it down, and shoved it back in the box. I was wasting my time. What was I even doing here? What would I have even said? My hands were shaking. There were too many possibilities. For once in my life, there wasn't a prank or a trick I could pull to fix the situation.

I slid the box back onto the shelf. I had to give Agent Mills an answer and I was running out of time. I leaned my head back against the boxes and sighed. Why did she choose me? She should have picked Oliss. He knew how to be an agent, how to fight and make up his mind. My skills seemed to only annoy people.

I figured it was time to leave before anyone questioned where I was. Before I got to my feet, I spotted a box on the shelf across from me. It read, **Instructors**.

I walked over to the box and pulled it off the shelf, kneeling on the ground next to it. Inside were records on all of the camp instructors. Agent Powell, Agent Willow, Agent Mills and all the others. I pulled Agent Mills' file out of the box. Okay, maybe this overstepped my welcome, but I didn't care. There were records about her family, where she was stationed, past cases, her relations with other agents. I stopped when a word caught my attention.

Under past cases, **Bayshire Stone Retrieval** stood out in big red letters. Not only was it her last case, but it was also the case that almost cost Agent Mills her job. I read through the mini case file. There was information about the Bayshire Stone, how dangerous it was. It was like a natural, oversized EMP generator. I read Agent Mills' notes about how the stone messed with the train she was traveling on. There was information about Mr. Bard and his history. A name caught my attention.

I looked up from the file. It all made sense now. I had to tell Alexis. There was no question about it anymore. I had to go with her. I had to save the T.S.O.

Chapter 41

Agent B

"Alexis!" I ran towards her. She was waiting by the road where the buses dropped us off.

"Decide to join me?" she asked. She smirked, then looked back at the empty road. "They will be driving up any moment."

"Alexis, I figured it out."

"Figured out what?"

I caught my breath and tried to make sentences out of the words floating around in my head. "I know how they did it, how they got into Headquarters, why we don't have any contact, what all the rumors about going public mean."

"You do?" She raised her eyebrows. "How? Who's 'they'?"

But before I could answer, a silver Toyota came around the bend of trees. The car kicked up dust in the road as it came to a stop.

"Hey!" Alexis smiled, and the passenger window lowered. A guy in the driver's seat smiled at her.

Alexis stepped up to the window. "Where's Watson?"

"Setting up a few more things. He'll be here soon."

Alexis sighed. "That changed our plans." This was Agent B, Tanner. The man on the other side of all the mysterious phone calls. "I'll meet you by the rock wall," she said. "Campers won't be there at this hour. Watson better get here soon."

Tanner nodded. "Copy that."

Agent B drove away. I followed Agent Mills through the camp towards the rock wall.

"What were you saying, Tony?" she asked.

"I might as well tell both of you at the same time."

Neither of us said anything when we reached the rock wall. Agent Mills turned away from it, frowning. The wall looked dangerous as I stood at the base of it, looking up to the top. The sun was starting to set and the glint off the top made it look ghostly in the shadows. Alexis was involving her friends while mine were back in Glayfield, probably in danger. It was aggravating, not knowing what was happening. What if they already figured it out? We could use their help.

A moment later, Agent B walked up.

The first thing I noticed was how Alexis relaxed as he walked closer, her frown turning into her relaxed sarcastic stare. These two had known each other for a while, but something was bothering both of them. I could tell in the way Agent Mills wouldn't stand still. She kept glancing at her partner then looking away. Something other than Ms. Blanchard and Headquarters was on her mind.

"This is Tony," Alexis said, waving her hand in my direction. Tanner nodded at me, but didn't say anything. "I thought Watson was coming with you."

"That was the plan," Tanner said. He looked irritated.

"So?" Alexis waited for him to answer.

"There was a mishap at the base. He had to help cover us and missed the plane. He should be here in a few hours."

No one said anything for almost a minute. Finally, Tanner spoke up.

"So, what's the plan?"

"We leave tonight," Alexis said, looking back and forth between us. "Watson has the coordinates for the safehouse, and he refused to share them with me, of course." She muttered that last part under her breath. Alexis had already filled Tanner in on everything that had happened so far. She explained that I knew Amelia and Emily, that they needed me on their team. I was itching to tell Alexis what I discovered. Everything was connected, but I couldn't get a word in.

"We can't take the cars," Tanner said. "The T.S.O. will be watching them. They have to stay here."

"Park around back. I'll tell Watson the same thing."

"Wait, we're not driving out of here?" I asked.

Tanner shook his head. "These cars can be tracked. It's safer on foot."

"What do you mean on foot?"

"You need to pack for a camping trip," Alexis said. "We're backpacking out of here. Dr. Powell will cover for us."

Tanner explained what was going on in Ohio. People were being told to stay out of the base. Others weren't allowed to leave. All vehicles were being monitored, so Tanner and Watson had both rented a car outside of the organization to get here. Those weren't safe either. Mr. Martial was super angry, and according to Tanner, threw a stapler at a wall after someone told him Ms. Blanchard went dark. Alexis smirked when Tanner said that part. No one knew what was going on. Mr. Bard was still off the radar.

"Tony says he figured it out," Alexis said, looking in my direction.

"Finally." I didn't mean to sound irritated, but it was hard not to. Tanner looked at me and Agent Mills crossed her arms. "It's the Bayshire," I said, everything I learned from the storage room was flowing through my mind. "Doom broke into Headquarters using the Bayshire. That's why we lost all contact. The thing is a natural EMP."

A light flickered in Agent Mills' eyes. "That makes sense," she said. "But what about Mr. Bard?"

I thought back to everything Agent Mills had told me about Mr. Bard. He owned the Bayshire Stone and was showing it across the country. It connected to what I learned in the storage room. There had been a name in Mr. Bard's files, a name that put everything together.

"Mr. Bard," I said, "is working with Jason Bakers, who you told me is Dr. Doom."

Alexis nodded, the gears in her brain moving.

"I went through your file. Jason Bakers is listed as one of his old contacts. They've been working together this whole time. We thought about it, but now we have proof. You said it was too easy. You were right. Mr. Bard gave Dr. Doom the stone." I paused, watching Tanner and Agent Mills for a reaction. They locked eyes with each other.

Dr. Doom had wanted the stone for his plan from the beginning. "If we can get into Headquarters undetected and remove the Bayshire from the area," I continued, "everything would go back online. We have to stop them from the inside. I just don't know what they want."

Agent Mills nodded, then she paused, looking right at me. "You went through my file?" Agent Mills asked.

"That doesn't matter right now," I said.

"Sounds complicated," Tanner said, ignoring Alexis.

"Good thing 'complicated' is what we do best," Agent Mills said. I smiled, which felt bad considering what we had to do next. "We leave as soon as Watson gets here, which better be soon."

Chapter 42

They Haven't Taught Us How to Lie Yet

After dinner, Agent Mills approached me on my way to my cabin. "After lights out, sneak out of your cabin," she said. "Meet me at the docks."

I finished packing, making sure I had stuff fit for camping this time. I had two sets of clothes, a flashlight, and a survival kit I found in my locker, which I hadn't looked through yet. It felt like fire was running through my veins. We were going to run away from camp and stop the bad guys. I took one more look in my locker. How were you supposed to pack for something like this? I squinted as something caught my attention. Sitting in the back of my locker was the second purple smoke bomb, the backup from when we pranked Agent Mills. I had forgotten all about it. I shoved it in my bag with everything else.

A while later I stared at the bunk above me, listening to Ethan and Handel laughing at something. But nothing felt funny to me anymore. I was a completely different person now. Despite my lack of training, I was a secret agent.

They called lights out over the loudspeaker. Handel and Ethan's conversation faded. Bentley put down the book he was reading. I waited, my backpack resting on the floor. Handel switched off the light as I rolled over in my bed. Now that it was dark out and everyone was supposed to be asleep, I felt wide awake. I couldn't calm myself.

An hour later, the sound of Ethan's snoring filled the cabin.

It was time to leave.

I slipped my shoes on, grabbed my bag, tiptoed across the wood floor. My fingers guided the door closed as I stepped onto the porch. I tiptoed down the steps and made it a few feet through the grass before I heard him.

"Going somewhere?"

I froze. It was Oliss. I spun around. He leaned against the open doorway. It was hard to tell in the dark, but I pictured the anger on his face.

"No?" I said. Why was I acting so stupid?

"Don't worry, I know what you're doing."

How was knowing that supposed to keep me from worrying? I was sneaking away from camp! In the middle of the night! "You do?" Had I given something away when we were sparring earlier? Or was he mad at me about the obstacle course for some reason?

"I was at the rock wall when you and Agent Mills showed up. Who's Amelia?"

"Why do you care?" I asked.

"Because I hate liars, and right now I can't tell if you're a good guy or bad guy." Oliss pushed himself away from the door and down the steps. The door clicked shut behind him as he stopped in front of me.

"Look, this is important," I said. "There is more going on than they are telling us. I'm helping Agent Mills."

"Everyone is always helping Alexis," he sighed. I didn't answer. What was that supposed to mean? I stepped closer to him. Despite his unsettling attitude, I needed Oliss to take me seriously.

"Whatever you know, you can't tell anyone. Not yet." I tried to make it sound severe, but I don't have the dramatic effect Alexis does.

"Why would I tell anyone?" Oliss asked.

A million reasons rushed through my head, but I wasn't about to give him any ideas. "Then why are you here?"

"To give you these." Oliss shoved a pair of glasses at my chest. No, not glasses. Night vision goggles.

"How did you get these?"

"I have my ways. We are training to be spies, are we not?"

I smirked. "Thanks."

"Get out of here. I'll cover for you. People will not be happy you left."

"Just another person you don't have to worry about."

"You got that right." I nodded at him, then turned and continued walking, slipping the goggles into the pocket of my bag.

When I reached the docks, Alexis and Tanner weren't the only ones there.

Chapter 43

Watson. Damien Watson.

The first thing I noticed was the hair. Somehow his buzzcut didn't match his face. The guy looked at me like I just spent the night in a dumpster or something.

"Alright, everyone's here," Alexis said. I kept my eyes on the new guy. "This is Agent Watson."

"You must be Tony," Agent Watson said. He shook my hand, firm and controlling. He glared at me. A fire burned deep in his eyes.

"Nice to meet you," I lied. I caught Tanner's smirk. I got the feeling they didn't really get along, and based on Alexis's stories about her last case, I was right.

"Mills, why do we need this guy?" Agent Watson asked, not taking his eyes off me.

I pulled out of his grasp. "Because," I said. "I know things you don't."

"Is that right?" Watson raised an eyebrow at me. "Mills, is he for real?"

"We need him, Watson, whether you like it or not. Deal with it. Are you guys ready?" Alexis asked. She kept looking back in the direction of camp.

"Ready," I said, readjusting my backpack.

If I wasn't mistaken, I thought I saw Agent Watson roll his eyes. "I do have a first name, you know. I'm not always just business."

"Sorry." Alexis gave a look I never wanted to be on the receiving end of. "Damien. Is that better?" Alexis said, annoyance staining her tone. There was definitely an odd connection between these three.

"The safehouse is about a day's walk southwest from here. But we'll have to stop at some point," Damien Watson said. It hadn't occurred to me what Alexis meant when she said pack for a camping trip. Part of me still wished we would have taken Tanner's car and disappeared down the road.

"Let's get going," Alexis said.

We headed towards the woods. I stepped into a steady pace beside Tanner. Alexis and Watson, or Damien I guess, were right in front of us. Despite feeling like ants were crawling down my back, I was in bright spirits. No matter how this ended, I was going to make sure Amelia was safe. And Emily. A day's walk through the woods. And we were starting in the middle of the night. Couldn't get any better, right?

Chapter 44

Angry Teachers are Scarier Than the Woods

Agent Watson led us through the woods for a solid two hours. We had flashlights in hand, but only turned them on when we really needed to. We didn't need people spotting us. Hardly any of us talked except for the occasional "watch out, there's a turn" or "dip ahead."

My feet were starting to hurt. Tanner was starting to limp, though he was trying to hide it. I thought of using my goggles from Oliss, but I didn't want to cause any problems if that wasn't allowed.

Another hour passed before Watson started slowing down.

"We can stop here," Alexis said. She didn't need to tell me twice. I dropped my backpack to the ground. "Let's set up camp. We should be far enough away by now. We'll give ourselves a few hours to sleep. Watson, Tony, we can take turns on guard duty." Tanner opened his mouth as if to protest, but Alexis cut him off. "No," she said. "You need to sleep. I don't need that leg slowing us down."

Agent Mills had running away down to a science. And here I was, digging through my survival kit like it was just another day at camp. Only this was the first time all summer I would be sleeping outside.

There wasn't a tent, but I did find a small bed roll in my survival kit. I laid it out on top of the dirt. There was a small metal tin and an empty water bottle. I found three packaged dried meals and a few granola bars. There was a small first aid kit and some matches.

If only we had covered outdoor survival or camping in Field Operations.

I sat on the bedroll with my backpack next to me. I had no water. I was tempted to pull out a granola bar, when Alexis said she would prepare food.

From her backpack Agent Mills pulled out a metal tin like the one I had, a packaged meal, and a bottle of water.

The tin unfolded into a pot. A T.S.O. gadget at its finest. She stuck the bag's contents inside and added some water. Damien brought over a pile of wood. He made a fire, and Alexis began cooking whatever was inside her pot.

Tanner set up his bedroll at the foot of mine, forming a square around the fire. He winced as he stretched out his leg, his muscles straining at the movement.

"How's your leg?" Alexis asked him before I could.

"Fine." He was obviously not fine.

"What happened?" I asked.

Tanner looked over at the others, but they started arguing about something, so they weren't paying much attention anymore. "Last mission," Tanner said. "Alexis tell you about the Bayshire Stone?" I nodded. "Well, I was on the field team when we first went after it. We were ambushed. Didn't end well."

I didn't pry anymore. Tanner seemed like a very private person.

"How exactly did you meet Alexis?" Tanner asked me.

163

I told him about meeting her at the rock wall after overhearing her story, about her picking me on the first day of combat class. When I told him about Alexis and her kick in my ribs, he chuckled. "That's Alexis."

"What about them?" I nodded in Damien and Alexis' direction.

Tanner laughed again. "What you see there is rare."

"How so?"

"Those two hate each other." I raised an eyebrow, but Tanner just smiled. "They were never friends, never got along. On Alexis' last mission they were kind of forced to be partners to get the Bayshire back to Ohio."

Alexis turned away from the food and pulled something out of her bag. When she turned around, Watson was reaching for the pot.

"Hey!" Alexis shouted at him. She grabbed his sleeve and pulled him away from it.

"What?"

"Leave it!"

"Make me!" Damien barked back at her. "I haven't eaten since I got on the plane."

"Why do you think I'm cooking?" Alexis retorted.

"Okay, I see your point," I said. I fiddled with my bed roll for another minute, listening to Agent Mills and Agent Watson argue about the food, about spending too much time in one place, and other things I didn't understand. "Do you ever interfere?" I asked.

"That would be a bad idea. I may be her partner and her friend, but there are some lines I don't cross." That made sense. I wouldn't want to be on Alexis' bad side. Ever. Watson was the enemy she was forced to tolerate, and Tanner was the guy who kept her in check.

Before Damien could say anything else, Alexis grabbed three small bowls and spoons from her bag and divided up the food.

Tomato soup. It was pretty good. She also handed out bottles of water. "Make it last," she said.

When everyone was done, Alexis took away the dishes. "I'll take first watch," Alexis said. No one complained. I turned away from the fire, but sleep wouldn't come.

I wanted to know what Emily and Amelia were doing. What would have happened if I stayed at camp? Why did Oliss help me? My cabinmates would notice I was missing when I don't show up for breakfast. Maybe it was a good thing Oliss had my back.

Chapter 45

I Play Watch Guard

Someone was shaking me. "Get up." It was Alexis.

"I'm up! Stop kicking me!"

Alexis stepped back and I sat up. "You've got the second watch. Wake Watson in an hour."

I looked at the dark sky through the trees. "What time is it?"

"About four-thirty in the morning."

"You were supposed to wake me half an hour ago." I climbed out of my bedroll.

"I know." I looked at Alexis. She gazed off into the forest.

"Just so you know, we haven't covered outdoor survival yet at camp."

Agent Mills sighed. "That's a year two thing. Okay, you're on guard duty. That means if you hear something suspicious or see something, you wake us up. Got it?"

"Got it."

Alexis walked to the other side of our camp. She was asleep as soon as her head hit the floor.

The fire was dying, small sparks glowing with the last bit of life. The moon peeked through the trees, providing me with light. An hour. I had an hour.

I watched the last of the orange flames in the fire dance across the wood. The forest was quiet, well, quiet from human activity. There was a buzzing rhythm up in the trees. All the bugs were still awake. The occasional flapping of wings made me jump. I added a piece of wood to the fire and watched it burn, the glow coming back to life.

I needed to keep myself awake.

I gnawed on one of the granola bars from my backpack. Take a bite. Look around. Chew. Swallow. Take a bite. Stare at the fire. Chew. Watch the others sleep. Swallow. Again, and again until it was gone.

I was tempted to throw the wrapper in the fire, but I stuffed it in my bag instead.

With nothing else to do, my mind drifted. Amelia and Emily were agents. Headquarters was under siege, meaning they could be in trouble. The director had disappeared and no one has heard from her. We didn't know what Dr. Doom or Mr. Bard were planning next, only that they were working together. The T.S.O. was at risk of being discovered. We didn't know how. Instructors were worried enough to shut down the camp. The Bayshire Stone was the cause of losing contact with Headquarters. Alexis thought I was important enough to be on her team. Tanner was injured, which meant we had to move slower than Watson wanted. Alexis and Watson hate each other. My granola bar was gone.

Only that last part seemed like my old reality, before I was told about the T.S.O., about camp.

I glanced at my watch. It was almost five in the morning. The night vision goggles from Oliss stared at me from inside the backpack. Should I have told Alexis about him? I pulled them out. The exact ones from Gadgetry class.

Everything looked green once I put them on. I could see Tanner, Damien, and Alexis all sleeping in their bedrolls. The trees towering over us looked ominous. The fire was slowly dying again. Something was moving through the forest about a mile off. Tanner rolled over in his sleep.

Something moving.

I tore off the goggles, but I could hardly see anything that far away. I put them back on. There it was. Something was coming towards us.

Chapter 46

This is the Part Where I Freak Out

"Get up!" I shouted. I stomped out the fire and tried to spread the ashes and the wood. "Wake up!"

Tanner stirred.

I threw the goggles at Alexis. "Hey!" She rubbed the side of her head as she sat up. Watson jerked awake.

"Something's coming." I pointed in the direction I saw movement.

Alexis fumbled with the goggles, looking where I was pointing. "He's right. Take it down!" she barked.

I rolled up my bedroll as fast as I could and stuffed it in my bag. In about a minute everyone was on their feet.

"Let's go!" Alexis said, shoving the goggles back in my hands.

We started running in the opposite direction of whatever was following us. I managed to get the goggles back on my face. Watson raced ahead of us, Alexis on his heels. Tanner was right behind me.

I looked back. Whatever was following us started picking up pace. It was a person. I could tell that much as it darted in between the trees. My heart was pounding, the sound of it beating filling my ears. I tripped on a tree root, regained my balance, and kept running.

"We're going the wrong way!" Watson shouted. He darted left and led us through the trees. We followed. Why did this have to happen on my watch?

"Keep going!" Alexis shouted.

I looked back again, but I couldn't see whoever was following us.

"I think we lost them!" I said, panting in between words.

But we didn't slow down. Damien made us run for another fifteen minutes before he slowed his pace.

"Whoever it was, we lost them," I said again.

Finally, Damien stopped running.

For a second all I could hear was the beating of my own heart as I caught my breath. "Everyone okay?" Alexis asked.

"Yeah." Tanner propped himself up against a tree. I bent over, hands on my knees.

"Who was that?" Watson asked. He hardly looked winded, just angry.

"I don't know," I said. I grabbed the water bottle from my pack and took a sip. It was difficult not to down the whole thing.

"Everyone take a moment. We'll keep going in about five minutes," Alexis said.

"We can't stop," Watson argued. "It's too dangerous."

Alexis sighed, and I prayed whatever came next was not a fight in the middle of the woods. "Look, we are all tired. And Tanner is still hurt. We need a moment."

"And who's fault is that?" Agent Watson mumbled to himself. But we all heard him. Alexis shook her head and sighed. She walked up to Tanner and had him sit down. Watson grumbled under his breath again. I stepped away from the group, wondering if I really should have come along. These three seemed so skilled, like they had been living undercover forever, and here I was trying to act like I was one of them. I walked until the trees covered most of my view of the group. I needed a moment to think about what was happening. I let my backpack slide off my shoulders.

"Tony!" Damien shouted. So much for being quiet.

I sighed. "Coming!"

And that was when something ran me into the ground.

Chapter 47

Welcome to the Club

My shoulder took the blow, hitting the ground first. A grunting sound escaped my mouth as pain inched through my arm and down my back. I was rolled over onto my backpack.

"Tony." My vision blurred, colors bouncing back into focus.

"Oliss?" He leaned over me. I couldn't read the expression on his face.

"What are you doing?" I groaned. Oliss grabbed my hand and hoisted me to my feet.

"Tony, what happened?" I heard Alexis' voice as she walked over to me. "Darwin, what are you doing here?"

"Yeah. Why did you tackle me?" I asked, grabbing my bag from the dirt. Tanner and Damien walked up behind Alexis, confused. Damien glared at Oliss.

"Darwin?" Agent Watson asked.

"I didn't want you to run off again," Oliss said.

"You were the one chasing us?" Watson asked. He looked like he wanted to hit him. At this point, I wouldn't have stopped him.

"Sorry," Oliss said. He didn't look sorry, just tired. "Listen, I can help you guys."

Alexis raised an eyebrow at him. "I'm not so sure that's a good idea."

"Look." Oliss stepped forward, the moonlight making his face look distorted and angry. "I am not my brother." Alexis raised an eyebrow, and I struggled to put together the pieces. Who was his brother?

"After Tony left, I couldn't sleep. I can't live in Miles' shadow. I won't. I'm a good agent, and I can prove it."

Miles was Oliss' brother? Miles, the friend Alexis said she couldn't trust anymore. No wonder Oliss was so bent on making a name for himself, on proving himself. That, I could understand.

Alexis sighed, hands on her hips. She was calculating her options. "Does anyone know you're gone?" she asked after a minute.

"No." Oliss shook his head. "I followed you guys about an hour after you left. Took me a while to find you."

Alexis shut her eyes, her head down. Then she started laughing, just a little bit. "Well, anyone who can surprise a spy shows they can help."

"Alexis," Damien sighed. "You can't seriously-"

"Yes, Watson, I can. Would you rather he find his own way back to camp at five in the morning and tell everyone we left? He isn't Miles." Alexis looked back and forth between us. "I'm his instructor, I know what I'm talking about." She sighed when her friends didn't rally with her. "Tony, what do you say?"

"Me?" Alexis nodded. Watson looked like his head was going to explode. Oliss glared at me. Despite his rock-solid attitude, I knew we needed him. I had no idea if we could trust him, but based on how he acted all summer, he was a team player. Being an agent was the most important thing to him. "We could use him." I nodded. "I say he comes."

"Then it's settled. Let's move out." Alexis walked past Damien. He opened his mouth to protest, but she shot a hand in his face and kept walking.

I looked at Oliss, who nodded at me. "Thanks," he said. I nodded, then followed Alexis. Agent Mills told me about moles in the organization. Technically, Oliss wasn't an agent yet, but I couldn't help but feel uneasy now that he was with us. I could only hope he was right about not wanting to be like his brother. Agent Watson took the lead again as we continued heading towards the safehouse. Oliss was filled in on everything that we knew, from Ms. Blanchard's meeting, Headquarters being attacked, and what we knew about the Bayshire. As Alexis explained everything to him, I kept my eye on him. She was right. We had to be careful who we trusted.

Chapter 48

No More Cell Phones

We each pulled out a granola bar and some water. We walked for almost four hours. Tanner handed a bar to Oliss.

Agent Mills paced back and forth, wringing her hands together. I sat on a rock, watching her. We had five or six hours left before reaching the safehouse.

"I have a question," I said. Everyone glanced at me, then turned away. "What do we do once we get there?" If I really thought about it, no one seemed to have a plan past getting away from camp. I knew we had to find the stone and get it out of Headquarters, but that didn't explain how to get in. "What are we going to do?"

Alexis huffed. "We're going to try and figure out where the stone is and remove it from Headquarters. Your job is to deactivate it. We don't know if people are trapped inside. We take down Dr. Doom and Mr. Bard. If they are in fact working together, we'll have our work cut out for us." I didn't like how vague that sounded, but at least Alexis had an idea of what we had to do next. She opened her mouth to say more, but something started buzzing.

"What's that?" Damien asked.

Alexis pulled a phone out of her backpack. She looked at the screen, bit her lip. "Miles," she said. I looked at Oliss, but he didn't even flinch. Agent Mills threw her phone against a tree. I jumped as it hit the bark, the screen shattering. Alexis picked up what was left of it and frowned. She took off the backing and pulled out the battery. Alexis threw the phone into the woods.

"What are you doing?" Oliss asked. Did Oliss know Alexis before he came to camp? The way she acted at the rock wall made me think not, but I wondered.

Alexis stomped on the battery then threw it in the opposite direction.

"Miles," Alexis started, a crazed look in her eye. "Oliss, do you know what he's up to?"

"I'm not really sure. He's just been talking about finally getting recognized, whatever that means."

"Seriously?" Alexis said. "You know, for someone who always said the rules came first, he seems pretty bent on ruining the T.S.O. just for some recognition. I can't believe he would let his ego control him."

"You have no idea how irritated he was when you were chosen as instructor," Oliss said.

"What?" Alexis looked at Oliss, and her thousand-pound shield seemed to drop.

"That's all I know," Oliss said. "He doesn't talk to me very much, other than to tell me I better work harder if I want to amount to anything."

"I thought he was my friend," Alexis said.

"We all did," Tanner said.

"It was one phone call!" Watson shouted. "You didn't have to break your phone." If he were a cartoon character, smoke would be flying from his ears right about now.

Alexis shook her head like that was the dumbest comment ever. "Damien, you know Miles. He could track a phone from the bottom of the ocean if he had the tech to do it. I can't have him tracking us. That was a new number. I don't know how he got it. Or how his caller ID showed up."

"Where did you get the phone?" Tanner asked.

"From base."

I nodded to myself. "If he had access to it, he could have done something to it before you got it."

"We've caught him sneaking around base and having phone calls he doesn't explain. He hasn't been acting like himself lately," Tanner said. Oliss didn't argue.

Maybe it was a good thing I didn't know this Miles Darwin. I was starting to see why having an outsider like me in the group might be helpful. There was no way I was corrupted by the enemy or the system.

"Sorry. I'm a little on edge at the moment," Alexis said. That was the understatement of the summer. "We're not trusting Miles right now. Not until I figure out what's actually happening." It seemed reasonable. "Anyone else have a phone on them?"

Tanner pulled a phone from his pack and did the same as Alexis, smashing the phone and tossing it. Agent Mills nodded at him, then turned to Watson. He glared at her, then seemed to give up his silent argument.

Agent Watson sighed. He pulled a phone out of his pocket. Before being told what to do, he pulled out the battery, dropped it, and smashed it under his boot. Then he threw it into the trees. "Happy?" he grumbled.

Alexis nodded. "Let's keep moving."

Chapter 49

Answers Would be Nice

We stopped an hour later for breakfast. Our packaged meals provided each of us with a serving of oatmeal. Not one of my favorites, but it was good enough. Better than just a granola bar. But what really got me moving was the bear.

We had just finished eating and were about to continue hiking when we saw it. It was far, but not far enough. As quietly as possible, Tanner spoke in a hushed voice, telling us to get moving before we had any problems. I had never seen a bear up close before, not in the wild. It was magnificent! The bear didn't seem to notice us. He kept eating, pawing at the grass at the base of a tree. We kept walking until we couldn't see it anymore, but it had me on edge even more than before.

So far, this hiking trip was turning out to be a lot more action-packed than I was expecting. I had seen Alexis and Damien bicker over food. I was tackled by a guy who was following us. I got to see Agent Mills smash her phone against a tree. When Alexis said we would run away, I was imagining a quick hike through the woods to this safehouse, not an all-night trek through bear infested woods.

We continued walking. After a while Oliss took over Tanner's backpack. I wondered why he chose to come help when he was still injured. He must really be devoted to working with his partner to hike through the woods on a healing injury.

"So, this Miles guy," I started. Alexis and Damien started arguing about something, I think it was about what type of bear we saw, so they weren't paying attention. Tanner looked at me like he was telling me it was a sensitive topic, but didn't ignore my question.

"He works with us in Ohio," he said.

"So, he's definitely a mole?" Oliss asked.

"We're not sure. But we're playing it safe. He's keeping something from us, from Alexis. You don't want to keep secrets from Agent Mills."

"And you just trust *her*?" Oliss asked.

Tanner sighed. "Alexis is my partner. We don't keep secrets. We don't keep information from each other. She and Miles have been good friends since camp. They are always training together. But when Alexis got back from her last mission, she overheard him on the phone with someone. People kept talking about Alexis going rogue because of what she had to do on her case, and Miles made it harder to tolerate.

"A while later she and I both started catching Miles in secret phone calls. He started keeping things from us, and it was obvious. He was never a good liar. He's good with tech. He's always been a rule follower. He can fight really well, but he can't lie."

"How do you think I learned about the T.S.O.?" Oliss said with a snicker. "Miles told me a lot more about the T.S.O. than I should have known." He shook his head. "You're right though. Before I left for camp, he kept talking about the world changing, about finally being noticed for all he's done. He went mad."

"We got about an hour left." Damien announced.

Relief kept me from collapsing. I didn't realize how tired my legs were, how sore my shoulders were from carrying my backpack.

"We just need answers," Tanner said.

"Yeah." I agreed. "We could use a lot of those right now."

Chapter 50

Welcome to the Safe House

The sun was above the trees now and the heat from its rays only made it harder to keep walking. It was a good thing we started so early in the morning before it got too hot.

"We're here," Damien said. There was a hint of relief in his voice. Maybe he was just as tired as I was. Maybe more considering all his arguments with Alexis.

Built in between the trees was a one-story building, the branches of the trees covering the roof entirely. You would never be able to see it from far away, or from the sky. It looked plain, a dark brown color that blended into its surroundings. All the windows were shut, with actual shutters preventing you from seeing inside.

We stepped up to the door. If you looked closely, you could see that the house was actually full of advanced security, not the old cottage it looked like from the outside. There were tiny security cameras in every corner.

Agent Mills stepped up to the door. She pushed the doorbell and a panel about as big as a hand slid out from the wall. Alexis placed her hand on it. A moment later it beeped and slid back into the wall.

"Identification," an electronic voice said.

"Agent Alexis Mills. Ohio base. Level four."

"Approved. Identification." The voice sounded oddly similar to Ms. Blanchard's.

I looked above the door. There was a small security camera perched on the wall. We were being recorded. It had to have some sort of voice-recognition software.

"Agent Damien Watson. Ohio base. Level three," Damien said.

"Approved." The voice repeated itself. "Identification."

Tanner spoke up next. "Agent Tanner B. Ohio Base. Level three."

I remembered the lesson we had about the seven levels in the T.S.O.

"Approved. Identification."

I didn't know what I was supposed to say, but Alexis opened her mouth before I could ask. "Tony Anderson. Agent-in-training. Level zero. Oliss Darwin. Agent-in-training. Level zero."

"Approved." I glanced at the camera again, curious if anyone was watching us. "Please insert verification."

"Do you have it?" Alexis asked.

Damien smacked his forehead. "No, I left it in Ohio," he said, sarcasm dripping like poison. He rolled his eyes, stepped up to the door, and pulled a key out of his pocket. It looked like a normal house key, but I knew better than to judge it so quickly.

Damien slid the key into the door lock.

"Code," the voice said.

"Forty-seven. Safehouse number Oh-eighty," Agent Watson said.

The door clicked and Damien pushed it open. We all stepped inside, and the door shut behind us. I could hear it click, locking us inside. Tanner slid two locks into place on the door. Alexis flipped a light switch, and the safehouse came to life.

"If we're so nervous about people knowing we left camp," I said, spinning in a circle to take in the room, "why did we just tell the T.S.O. we got here?"

Watson dropped in backpack and looked at me. "All safehouses are on a closed circuit. You can't access any information about who is using them or when unless you are authorized by a director."

"So no one knows we're here?" I asked.

Alexis shook her head. "No one knows except Ms. Blanchard, and no one knows where she is. No one else can get in since we have all been approved. It's perfectly safe."

The place was a lot bigger than it looked. A living area was set up to the right with a large couch, a coffee table, TV, and fireplace. Off to the left was a hallway. The other side of the room had a giant dining table. A closed door waited to be opened behind the table.

"This is nice," I said. The floor was tiled. The windows were shut, the lights on the ceiling brightening the entire room. Next to the front door was a huge panel with a bunch of buttons and switches. This place was buzzing with electricity.

"Everybody, wash up," Alexis said. "There's a bunch of rooms down the hall, each with its own bathroom. There should be some clothes in there too. Freshen up, get some rest."

Chapter 51

The Grand Tour

After spending the night in the woods, it felt good to take a hot shower, to be clean. The shower was amazing, the bedroom spotless. I threw on a clean T-shirt and jeans and switched out my shoes with a pair of field boots I found in the closet. There were five different sizes to choose from. A laptop computer and a cell phone sat on the dresser. There was also a black bag, but I didn't touch it.

This place had to have everything. I left the bedroom, my backpack thrown on the bed, and headed down the hall. Everything on this side of the house looked like living quarters. I opened the door on the other side of the dining table.

It was a completely different section of the safehouse. There was a huge kitchen with another lounge area and TV. A walk-in pantry was stocked with nonperishable food in the kitchen. A door led outside, but it was locked, just like the front door. I turned the corner.

"Wow."

An entire computer system filled the space. A row of computers, two large screens on the wall. A table filled with metal boxes. The whole place looked too clean to enter. But someone else already had.

Alexis sat at one of the computer screens.

"What are you doing?" I asked.

"Setting up the database. Logging into the system." I walked over to her. "The T.S.O. has what's called the T.S.O. database. Access to any information you want across the world. I set up the safehouse computer system, activating all outside security systems. It's a closed network, so you can only access the surveillance from these computers. Hopefully we'll be able to find the director's exact location once it's all set up and running. And we should be able to find the Bayshire using a specified energy sensor. This place hasn't been used in a while, but it's all up to date."

"What's through there?" I pointed to a door on the opposite side of the room.

"The garage. It's pretty cool. Check it out." Alexis looked back at the computer, not paying attention to me anymore.

I hadn't noticed a garage outside. I opened the door.

The garage was bigger than the living room. There were three cars, four motorcycles, and a huge storage compartment. Bikes hung on the wall. A table was set up on the opposite side of the room. Various objects filled half the workspace.

Standing by the table was Oliss. "Pretty cool, isn't it?"

"More than cool. This entire place is awesome."

"My dad's a mechanic," Oliss said. "I wanted to check out the cars." I walked over to him.

Then I noticed a completely separate section of the garage. There was an alcove in the corner. From where I stood, I could see a blue mat on the ground, but nothing else.

It was probably a gym or combat room. Of course this place had one.

"Why exactly did you follow us?" I asked, reverting my attention back to Oliss.

"Like I said. I want to help. Same as you."

I had never been a part of something this important. Before summer I would have never been caught doing something like this.

"You know what Ethan would say if he was here?" I asked, trying to lighten the mood. What was everyone doing back at camp, I wondered. They would notice by now that we were missing. Were they looking for us?

"Why should I care?" Oliss messed with some different tools on the table. "Come on," he said. "Let's find something to eat."

We all made sandwiches in the kitchen. Tanner propped up his leg and iced it while he ate.

"Did you guys see your gadget kits yet?" Alexis asked us.

"Already went through everything," Watson said. Tanner nodded.

"Gadget kits?" I asked. Oliss looked just as interested.

"The black bag in your rooms," Alexis clarified. I shook my head. Was that bag full of gadgets? I finished my sandwich and raced down the hall to my room. I heard the TV turn on, the news channel blaring from the kitchen. Alexis still had the database searching for the Bayshire's heat signature to verify it was in Headquarters as well as Ms. Blanchard's location. I shut the door to my room to muffle the noise from the television and opened up the bag.

There were more than just gadgets. Inside the bag I pulled out one item after another. A set of pens. I thought of the pens from Gadgetry class and wondered which one was which. A pair of night vision goggles and sunglasses. The night vision goggles were bulkier than the pair I brought with me. There was a wallet. Inside the wallet was a bunch of cash and a few credit cards. There was a pack of gum too. A small black box caught my attention, and I opened it. Inside was a pair of what I thought were two very small security cameras. There was also a set of earbuds and a few other things.

But what made me stop and think was the cellphone on the dresser. I turned it on, finding it full of programs I didn't recognize. I would have to play with those later.

Amelia and Emily came to mind. Who knows what kind of trouble they were in. I looked at the closed door. It wouldn't hurt to call them, would it? I needed to know they were okay. Alexis was paranoid about phones being tracked, but it was provided for me in the bag. It had to be safe. Right?

I couldn't wait any longer to talk to my friends. It was like an ache that wouldn't go away. I looked at the phone, tracing my thumb over the button. Giving it one last thought, I made the call.

Chapter 52

Forbidden Phone Calls

"Hello?"

My heart skipped a beat. She actually answered. "Amelia? This is Tony."

"Tony? This is Emily."

"Emily? What are you doing with Zegro's phone?" The sound of Emily's voice helped me relax. She was okay.

"Amelia left the room for a moment, so I answered. What's going on?"

The words got lodged in my throat. What a casual question. "A lot more than you would think," I said.

"Try me," Emily laughed over the phone, but she sounded a little distracted.

"Remember how I said I was going to camp?" I asked. I told her about being recruited by Ms. Blanchard for the T.S.O. and going to the training camp. I told her about Alexis and how she said she knew them. I told Emily about Doom escaping from prison and the Bayshire being stolen. I told her about running away.

The line was silent when I finished talking. I wanted her to say something. Anything that would tell me she was paying attention and didn't think I was crazy.

"So, you're telling me you know about the T.S.O.?" she asked.

"Yes."

"And you know Amelia and I are agents, and you're actually working with Agent Mills? This isn't just another one of your pranks?"

"Yes. I mean, no. This isn't a prank," I managed to spit out. "How would I even know all this stuff, Emily?"

"I was not expecting that!" Emily started laughing over the phone, but I didn't see what was so funny. She sighed, the excitement subsiding.

"Listen, we need your help, you and Amelia." I didn't mention the others don't know I called.

"Tony, um, I should probably confess something," Emily said.

"What?"

"Amelia isn't here." Her voice cracked.

"What do you mean she's not there? You have her phone."

"Look, Amelia and I have been working on a case. And we've suspected Ms. Blanchard was up to something for a while. We've been watching her. We know she's not the bad guy here. She just wants the T.S.O. to stay secret."

"What about Amelia?"

"She was at Headquarters yesterday. I haven't heard from her since. It's been radio silence. No one's allowed in or out. I don't know what's going on."

All the blood in my body must have dissolved, because everything went cold. Amelia was trapped in Headquarters. She was being held hostage by the man who wanted her dead.

"Tony?"

"I'm here. Listen, we're on our way. We have a plan, sort of. Keep this number and I'll call you when we get moving," I said.

"You're going to need the director's help," she said. "I'm not sitting out on this one either."

I nodded. "We're trying to locate Ms. Blanchard now. We'll need all the help we can get." The others wouldn't be happy about this, but I didn't care. Besides, not a single person in my group worked at Headquarters. They wouldn't know the ins and outs of the place. Emily did.

"And Tony?" I waited for Emily to say more. "I'm glad you know about the T.S.O. Amelia will be too." I smiled.

Chapter 53

Time to Save the T.S.O.

I hung up the phone, my blood racing with the idea of actually being able to stop some real criminals. Emily was safe. Amelia was in danger. This is why I was here.

I threw the phone on the bed and thrust open the door. Damien leaned against the door frame, glaring at me. Uh-oh.

"I knew we couldn't trust you," he growled. Agent Watson grabbed my arm and dragged me down the hall.

"Hey!" I shouted. "Listen!" I pulled my arm out of his grasp.

Damien raised his voice and yelled at me. "I just listened to you tell someone everything we know! How am I supposed to *not* think you're a traitor?" The others walked in from the kitchen. I swallowed. This guy was unsettling when he was angry.

"What's going on?" Alexis asked.

"This kid just told someone all our information."

"First of all," I said, smoothing down my shirt. "I am not a kid. And secondly, I was talking to an ally."

Damien glared at me. Sure, I wasn't a good fighter, and I had only known about the T.S.O. for a little while. But I was finally a part of something important. I was useful. Talking to Emily made me realize that. I couldn't let other people keep pushing me around.

"Explain," Alexis said. She looked flustered, her ponytail a little too tight.

"I was talking to Emily."

"I told you to let them be." Alexis took a step forward. I couldn't tell if she was angry or oddly proud that I disobeyed her orders.

"And if I did, we wouldn't know that Agent Z is trapped in Headquarters with everyone else." Everyone stared at me. I didn't mean to yell. I was never allowed to yell at home, but I couldn't stop myself. I took a deep breath, lowered my voice, and continued. "Emily and Amelia have been watching Ms. Blanchard for a while. We need the director's guidance and Emily's help if we're going to find a way in."

"It's too dangerous to bring anyone else into this," Damien huffed.

"Agent Steinfeld and the director know their way around HQ. We don't. If we're going to take back Headquarters and save the T.S.O. we need all the help we can get," I said.

"He's right," Oliss said.

Damien looked like he wanted to argue, but he kept his mouth shut. I looked at Alexis. No one had to say anything to know she was in charge here. She had the final say. We couldn't do this on our own, and she knew it. To not take this chance and seek out Emily and Ms. Blanchard would be a colossal mistake.

"Well?" I asked.

Agent Mills shook her head and smiled. "Well, I guess we have a new mission," she said.

I didn't break, nor did I show how relieved I was that she agreed. There would be no more pranking people to get attention, no more trying to be something I wasn't. I was recruited to be a secret agent, and I was going to save the T.S.O.

Join the T.S.O. agents in the final chapter
of their adventure in:

A Hostage in Headquarters

Coming Soon

Have you read the first two books in the T.S.O. series? Don't miss the rest of Agent Mills and Agent Z's other adventures.

Finding Doom   *The Bayshire*

Acknowledgements

This story has been waiting patiently (and sometimes not very patiently) to be published as I took a pause in writing to experience the many milestones life has thrown at me. Since 2021 when *The Bayshire* was published, I graduated both high school and college. I moved across the country. I transferred to Maryville College where I received my Bachelor's in ASL/English Interpretation. I've made many new friends along the way. *Recruited* got put on the backburner between homework assignments, internships, moving, helping on my family's new homestead, and buying my first home. So first, I want to thank each of YOU who have been waiting so patiently for this book. You have been so patient with me in continuing the T.S.O. adventure. Thank you!

I want to thank Chelsea Fuchs, who has always been an amazing editor and teacher. You also waited patiently for me as I impatiently started, stopped, and restarted my own timeline. This book has been through multiple rewrites and scene changes. Tony would not be the character he is without my amazing editor's suggestions, critiques, and support.

A huge thank you to all my beta readers, especially Abby and Rebecca. Your suggestions, critiques, support and feedback helped put the finishing touches together.

My family has been by my side not only during the making of this book, but during everything. We have been through so much these past years, but you still stick by me. Mom, thanks for the endless phone calls where I ramble about my books and stress about their incompleteness. You mean more to me than words can say. Audrey, my wonderful sister, thank you for matching my craziness and listening to me go on and on as I worked out my plots and backgrounds. To my favorite brother Dominic, thank you for your awesome book cover modeling, and Abby for all your suggestions and beta reading tips. Joanna, keep writing your stories. One day our book will be read by everyone else! Dad, thanks for always supporting me and guiding me while letting me also make my own mistakes. I wouldn't be who I am without all of you.

"Whatever you do in word or deed, do all in the name of the Lord Jesus, giving thanks through Him to God the Father."
-Colossians 3:17

About the Author

R.E. Klinzing resides in the mountains of East Tennessee. Author by night, she spends her days working as an ASL Interpreter. Her free time is spent reading, watching movies, coloring, and enjoying outdoor fun like paddleboarding and hiking. R.E. Klinzing hopes to inspire young writers to pursue their stories and goals while igniting a love for learning and reading in every person that opens a book.

Follow her on Instagram and Facebook at
@reklinzing_authorofficial
Learn more at reklinzing.com
https://reklinzing.com

www.ingramcontent.com/pod-product-compliance
Lightning Source LLC
Chambersburg PA
CBHW020556250626
47154CB00004B/1248